BIG Secrets Everywhere

Stories by Jeanne Althouse

ISBN: 978-1-945917-83-7

Printed in the United States of America

Cover design: Tracey Capobianco
Cover art: Cerca Con Google Silhouette Arte

Also by Jeanne Althouse:
Boys in the Bank, Redbird Chapbooks, 2018
Wrinkle in the Brain, Chapbook, 2012

"Making other books jealous since 2004"

Big Table Publishing Company
San Francisco, CA
www.bigtablepublishing.com

For Calvin,
Rhys, and Westley

Table of Contents

Part I: Secret Children

Love Child   11

Stand Up   18

Confession   20

#theprocedure   31

Big Lies   34

Part II: Sins and Regrets

Cool Shirt   39

Caught in Headlights   40

Sin of Omission   46

A Conversation Between Two Sisters with a Hawk Watching   48

Toccata and Fugue   51

Part III: Secret Desires

Parallel Octaves   59

Echo of Exploding Bombs   63

Interrupted Play   66

Calming Properties of Ice Cream   68

Surprising Effect of a Dewy Grass Bath   73

Part IV: Ultimate Mystery

Ghosts in the Grand Wardrobe   87

Fallen Star   92

Birds on the Water   94

Miles to Go   97

Ultimate Mystery   101

"We dance round in a ring and suppose,
but the secret sits in the middle and knows."

~ Robert Frost, "The Secret Sits"

Part I: Secret Children

Love Child

She inherited my uncle's face. She inherited his pale skin, freckled nose, smoky eyes, narrow cheek bones, the way he tilted his head to his left when he spoke. She inherited his love of gab and tendency to lecture. She inherited his profession and his talent at chess. She inherited many things from Uncle Norm, but not his name.

I didn't believe in religion, in transitions to the other side, in seeing people after death. But the first time I met Renata Taylor that changed.

We faced each other in a booth at Plant Gourmet, the restaurant in San Francisco where she suggested we meet for lunch. She smelled of smoke. Was it her, or the smoke rising from the restaurant's grill? I looked across the booth at her, at my uncle's face. I doubted she was a smoker, but she looked so much like him that I expected her to raise a cigarette to her lips.

Uncle Norm was a lifelong smoker; he died ten years ago of lung cancer. He never had children, never wanted any, he said. So, who was this woman?

"What does she want?" my husband, Nick, asked me in the car on the way to our meeting. Nick, a lawyer, specializes in estate planning, has an eye for inheritance issues. "Does she want money?"

Nick would never submit his DNA sample to an ancestry testing service. He argues that, regardless of their promises you have no control over what they do with the information. The databases are subject to hacks and the information can be used against you. He rants about DNA testing with "Remember that serial murderer they called the Golden State Killer? The feds found him using a DNA match."

He'd go on talking for ages on this subject if I let him. His enthusiasm *against* the testing shows me that secretly he's fascinated with the possibilities. Smoldering inside Nick is a badass longing to flame up. Don't tell, but it's one reason I married him. I've got that badass inside too. That, and my curiosity about ancestors, made me get the test without telling him. When my results revealed this unexpected cousin and she contacted me, Nick, too, was interested. He spent more time reviewing the test results than I did.

Inside, waiting to be seated, I held out my hand. "I'm Emma," I said. "Are you Renata?"

She looked German, pale skin, like mine. I guessed she was a couple of years older than I was. Early fifties maybe. She wore a blue knit dress I recognized from the latest Bowden catalog, expensive, dressy. She brought her husband too, second husband she told us later, Chadwick. Chad was Black, dressed in a white shirt, charcoal suit coat over jeans, no tie. Classy. I guessed he was at least ten years younger than she was. Good for her: a younger man, takes confidence, I thought. He sat quietly, arm around her. Supportive. I liked him immediately, but I wasn't sure about her.

"I'm not going to make small talk," she said, after we ordered. She stared at me with Uncle Norm's smoky, dreamy eyes. I took a deep breath. The idea that Uncle Norm had a daughter was difficult to absorb. I considered not telling her. I hardly knew this woman I reminded myself.

Renata touched my hand across the table. I hate being touched by strangers, but I tried not to move my arm away. My eyes strayed over to Nick. He looked as surprised as I was to see the family resemblance, but if she asked for something, I could hear his *I told you so*.

Renata leaned forward. "I'm going to be frank with you," she said.

I was worried, thought here it comes, a request.

"It's fine if you stare at me. Go ahead," she said.

Her eyes locked mine in a contest over who would look away first. (I looked away first. I lost these contests with Nick too.)

"I want to know," she said. "Do I resemble anyone in your family?"

Yes, yes, I thought, but I didn't answer. Would this discovery come to harm us?

The silence stretched out. The waiter, a young man wearing a Plant Gourmet tee, offered us more water.

Renata turned to Chad, searching for help. He squeezed her shoulders, winked at her. I liked Chad.

She went on, encouraged by him. "I'm adopted. I never met my birth mother or father; I don't know who they are. It's hard to explain to someone who is not adopted, but in school other kids got to talk about how they looked like their mom or dad. I never got to look like anyone in my family."

She had a yearning in her voice, a plea for understanding. I decided to tell her. Nick often accused me of being a softie. I argued it made me good at my job as a therapist. I could empathize.

Yet I stuttered when I answered, and I haven't stuttered since college. "Yes. Ah…yes," I said. You remind me of Uncle Norm." There, I did it. I can't take it back now.

"Who was Uncle Norm?" she said.

"He was my mother's brother. Happily married to Aunt Marilyn, we thought, but who never had children." The "we thought" hangs in the air while I wonder if Aunt Marilyn knew about this. She said she agreed with him that they didn't want children. She died soon after Uncle Norm, so I'll never know if she knew. Did my mother know this about her brother? She never said and she died last year. My grandparents and parents are gone; I am an only child so there's no sibling to ask.

Lunch arrived. We started eating but she ignored her plate. Her next speech gushed out of her mouth as if she'd been rehearsing it for days. She explained her name. Renata, after Renata Tebaldi, a famous opera singer. Her adopted mother liked opera and liked that the name meant *reborn*. Renata explained how happy she was growing up; she knew she was adopted, from a Catholic charity, and was made to feel "chosen."

My brain fired up with questions. A love child? A Catholic charity? We were not a Catholic family and Uncle Norm wasn't religious. I remember Mom said she volunteered as a cleaner at a Catholic home during college; she claimed her place promised every unwed mother complete anonymity in the adoption process. *Love child. Unwed mother.* Loaded terms from the past. Mom liked to tell me how values had changed since her generation, how pregnancy without marriage no longer contained the shame it once did.

I felt tears close as I missed Mom all over again. "What do you do for a living?" I asked, hoping to shift onto a less emotional topic.

She said, "I teach high school history. Chad teaches English. We met at San Francisco Unified."

My mouth fell open. "Uncle Norm was a teacher too—the same subject, high school history."

"That's interesting," she said, smiling. "I must have the history teacher DNA."

She was making a joke, but I was digesting the coincidence. After an awkward silence, Nick jumped in, bless him. "Emma's uncle taught history decades ago; it's pretty different now I bet."

"Yes," she said, shifting into lecture mode, "In your uncle's time we considered one narrative as the true history of the United States. Teachers used one history textbook, usually with a Euro-centric perspective, mostly British."

I notice she said, *your uncle's time* and not *my father's time.*

"For example, older textbooks described Jamestown as the first permanent settlement in the United States, but we know there were earlier settlements. For decades they weren't mentioned in the history narrative because the British defeated France and Spain prior to the American Revolution, and the winners write history. The way I teach today in high school is to supplement with original sources, like letters, old newspapers, so the students get diverse interpretations and learn to form their own opinions."

Chad and Nick have finished their lunch, but her food sat half eaten.

"History is constantly being revised as we get better science and make new discoveries. Just recently the DNA from an ancient horse tooth solved the mystery of the Chincoteague wild ponies—and confirms they descended from Spanish horses marooned on Assateague Island sometime in the sixteenth century."

Odd she mentioned that example. Uncle Norm loved his horses. When I was growing up, he kept a roan mare at a ranch outside of his small town. He liked to adopt old horses and rescue them from slaughter.

Nick squirmed in his seat next to me. I raised my hand as if we are in class and I'm impatient to be called on.

She smiled, obviously has a good sense of humor. "I know I talk too much," she said.

"That's an understatement," said Chad, grinning, squeezing Renata's shoulders again. "But she's a fantastic teacher."

Nick and I smiled at each other. He liked Chad too.

My mind ignited, on fire with the big questions I didn't ask: What happens when we have to revise our *family* history? Who *was* Uncle Norm? *Do we really know anyone*? I needed to change the subject again, to buy time for calming down. "Do you, by any chance play chess?"

Uncle Norm was the 'fun uncle,' knew how to party, liked to play a prank, loved to tell a joke, taught us all chess. Every year, when he came to visit, he arrived with a different hair look, or a changed beard style. He always brought his chess set.

"She's a genius at chess, an attacking maniac on the board," said Chad.

"I adore chess," she said. "I guess I got the chess DNA too."

Everyone laughed.

Over dessert we talked more, about our lives, our work, our families. I explained what I knew of my uncle's medical history. Chad and Nick got deep into a discussion of fishing and debated which brand was the best rod threading device. Renata and I figured out how old Uncle Norm would have been in the year she was born—he was twenty, in college, not married, had not yet met Aunt Marilyn. That was a relief; I did not want to think of him betraying my aunt.

After lunch we slid out of the booth and exchanged friendly hugs. Nick could tell I was absorbed and emotional and he offered to drive. As we sat in the car, I looked back at Renata, getting in her car with Chad. My feelings were strong, but ambiguous. The revision of my family history was like a loss of innocence, a hard reminder that people you love are complex, mysterious, full of surprises, not always good ones. Yet meeting my cousin was also a gift, having a part of Uncle Norm return, remembering his face, our good times together. Would we become friends? Would we become family? I felt the warmth of her hug and, on my hands, the hint of her smoky scent, lingering.

But Nick did not start the car.

"Can we talk?" he said.

"Of course." I waited. We watched Chad and Renata drive away, waved a friendly goodbye.

"It was uncanny to see Uncle Norm's face on her," Nick said. "I went to a few wild parties in college; I could have a few mystery children around myself…"

Nick was making a joke—trying to cheer me up. "That's not funny," I said.

"Seriously, your uncle may not have known about the pregnancy. Isn't that a relief? If he'd known he'd have helped with the pregnancy—he wouldn't just abandon some girl he got pregnant, would he?"

He reached across the console, took my hand.

"On the other hand, there's no doubt Renata's related to someone in your family."

"Someone?" I asked.

"She *could* be Uncle Norm's child," he said. "But…maybe not."

What did he see that I missed?

"Her hands, the long narrow fingers. And she was left-handed…"

I was a leftie; got that from Mom.

In the silence that followed, we were both thinking about the DNA results.

Two people who shared a percent of DNA match are *most likely* cousins, the voice in my brain argued. But the amount of shared DNA is not exact. DNA results fall on a spectrum. In rare instances two people could be…"

"Half siblings," said Nick, completing my thought.

I held my breath, trying to make sense of it.

Was she Mother's love child?

Stand Up

When I was six, Ma said my job with my baby brother Milo was to get the giggles out. I rushed in the door after school each afternoon, anxious to help Milo release the pressure of his trapped giggles that Ma said had built up like bubbles of stomach gas and had to be popped. As he crawled away on the rug, I grabbed a stuffed dog and chased him, barking. I caught him, turned him over, and blew zerberts on his belly, but he had a serious nature and it was hard work to raise a laugh.

My aunt, who transported me to and from school said, "He ain't laughing 'cause he ain't got a father." She glared at my mother. "Milly can't keep a man around here."

Our family was Milly, Milo and me, Marcus. And Aunt Jules who went to work at the Piggly Wiggly so Ma could care for Milo. My mother's childhood with Jules, her older, jealous half-sister, left her determined to teach me to be a good brother.

"I'm the man around here," I said to Milo. I stood as tall as I could, pointed my finger at the bedroom and said, "Go to your room young man and don't come out until you're ready to giggle."

Milo pushed himself up to his sitting position, stared at me for a long minute, pausing as he did when he was taking a pee in his diaper, then burst out laughing, smiles all over his pretty face.

As we grew older, at family parties, the aunts, ladies who weren't anyone's sister that I knew of, fawned over Milo's blonde curls, his wide eyes like Ma's eyes, and chubby cheeks, while the men, who we were told to call uncles, sorry for my plain face, took me outside to throw a baseball around. They said, wasn't it odd I looked so much like Uncle Bill? Uncle Bill had a square jaw, a balding head, and smelled like cigars, but ever since he danced on top of the backyard picnic table during a birthday party for Ma, I adored him. He would do anything I asked: serve ice cream for breakfast, hold a spoon on his nose for three minutes, or carry a Whoopee cushion in his back pocket for surprising everyone when we sat down to supper. Before he left, he built my fourth grade Mission Project and said it was okay to tell the teacher I did it.

Into high school my brother's serious nature raised the bar for me and I had to work much harder to get laughs. No more knock-knock jokes: I had to develop full-on comedy routines. By then Uncle Bill had moved away, and Ma suggested I sign up for an improvisation workshop after school. Aunt Jules called me a show-off, but Ma said I could be a professional actor someday.

I went to college on a church scholarship, but dropped out after a year. I yearned to work the comedy clubs; I needed the stimulation of a mike in my hand. When I look out from the stage, at the people sitting at tables, nursing a beer or a whiskey, a lonely old man, or two ladies together, heads bubbling up out of the smoky darkness, the smell of nuts, beer and sweat in my nose, I feel the desperation, the pressure inside them, the ache of sadness, swelling up like gas. We all need laughs to get through a lonesome Sunday, or over a lost love—or wondering who our father is.

Confession

When he died, their father had two requests. He wrote these last wishes on pale blue stationery from 47 Park, the exclusive London hotel in Mayfair where he took them the summer after their mother died, to celebrate her life in a place she loved. They recognized the fine point line of his favorite black pentel pen, the arches and big loops, distinctly his. They imagined him taking the blue hotel paper out of his home office desk drawer where he saved it as memorabilia from the trip, the stationery never before used, and, as was his habit, leaning over the blank page, his left elbow bent, holding the weight of his chin on his hand, pausing to think carefully before he began to write.

Dear Simon and Sophie: By the time you read this, I hope I have had the courage to tell you in person and it will not come as a surprise to you. I begin by saying that Louise was and remains the love of my life, and whatever I did in that one moment with a woman I hardly knew meant nothing compared to the life we shared with you children.

Their father did not have the courage—or the time—to tell them. The children, in shock and grief, were reading their father's note at the law offices of McGill and Cook two weeks after his unexpected death. Simon stared at the hand-written note which had been attached to the formal printed document titled "Last Will and Testament of Garridan S. Sims." The familiar handwriting slammed him with the complicated emotions he associated with being his father's son: admiration, awe, frustration, embarrassment, envy, guilt, regret. At twenty-nine, his life looked stalled and inconsequential compared to his father's accomplishments. Simon's mind filled with memories of his father—his eccentric love of Holland Lop rabbits, the way his fingers smelled of Black Cavendish tobacco and when you mentioned it, he claimed he hadn't smoked pipes for years, the parchment-thin feel of his cheek when Simon kissed him goodbye after the family dinner, not knowing it was the last.

"I'm so sorry about your father," Jack Cook had said when they arrived. A man in his seventies with a round, kind face, who had known the children for years, he reached for Simon's hand, but caught himself, paused—they touched elbows instead. "Even with that mask on, Simon, you're the spitting image of Gary. You've got his dark hair, that serious brow, and those deep blue eyes. It's the deep blue of the male Indigo Bunting. Rare in human eyes." Cook's favorite vacation was a birding tour with his birdwatching group, the Twitchers; he saw the world in the colors of his birds.

"You, young lady," he said, nodding at Sophie. "You've got your mother's eyes. Reminds me of the Chestnut Bunting. Warm brown. So sorry. So sorry about your dad."

A loan officer had found the body of Gary Sims at his desk at work, head resting on his folded arms as if he had dropped off to sleep. As President of the local credit union, traditional and conservative, who wore a suit at work even on casual days, afternoon naps were something he would never imagine doing in public. The doctor said it was a heart attack; sudden and fast. Simon wondered if Dad knew death was coming. He'd recovered from COVID, a serious case which kept him in the hospital and on a ventilator for days, but it had been six months since his illness and he claimed he felt fine. Did his father have a premonition and that's why he wrote this farewell script?

I meant to tell you when your mother died, but I lacked the courage to confess, afraid it would forever change the way you think of me.

The letters refused to stay in focus for Simon. He closed his eyes, tried to believe that it wasn't a dream, sitting there in the glaring lights of the McGill and Cook conference room at their laminate table which felt cold as stone to the touch of his extended, sweaty palm. Simon's days, shrunk by the pandemic, were defined by boring routines in his small condo, alternating with runs at the local park— and he had difficulty finding any joy to look forward to. He hadn't been touched by a woman since before COVID struck. Since his father died, mornings he would lie in bed watching the sliver of light under his window shade go from dim to glare as the sun rose.

I realized after I survived near-death with COVID, fate could deliver something else, and without me, no one would be watching over Kasper.

Kasper? Simon did not recognize that name. A friend of his dad?

"Kasper? Who is Kasper?" asked Sophie. Her voice was a whisper. She was a year older than Simon, but had always been the shy one, had always let him lead. When she was in elementary school, she developed an aversion to touch and was diagnosed with mild autism, but she managed well and most people she met didn't notice. An art major in college, she loved to draw and brought a sketch pad everywhere with her. Before California mandated COVID sheltering in 2020, Simon and Sophie each lived separately, but, afraid of COVID, afraid to be alone, Sophie had moved in with Simon. Two years later, in his two-bedroom condo, they still opened their laptops every morning, put on headphones, and sat at his kitchen table, working. She designed web sites for Artcloud.com which helped galleries and artists sell online, and he, a certified hypnotherapist specializing in weight management, guided his patients on Zoom. His patient load had increased during the pandemic, with many people dealing with stress by eating for comfort.

He moved his chair closer to Sophie.

I met Sharee LaBrowne at a company function. She was the lead singer in a band, popular at the time. There really are no excuses for what I did. Our baby boy had Down Syndrome with complications and he wasn't expected to live. Kasper surprised his doctors; he's an adult now. I am not proud of my betrayal, but I am grateful to know Kasper; he's been a treasure in unexpected ways.

Sophie said, "Dad had a secret son? Unbelievable."

"I know," said Simon. This changed everything he had ever thought about his perfect father, everything he had cherished as family history, everything he thought was true. For Sophie's sake he hid his shock under a breezy tone: "I could handle something typical of Dad—that he gave our inheritance to SaveABunny, or made us promise monthly visits to Aunt Elma, or went all philosophical on us, like 'always be kind' or 'wear clean underwear every day in case you're in an accident'—but this?"

"That was Mom," said Sophie. "She said the bit about clean underwear."

"I really miss her," said Simon. Their mother had died of ovarian cancer, a year before COVID started. They said it was good she missed the pandemic.

"I miss her too," said Sophie. "But this? How could he hide this from Mom?"

Cook cleared his throat and looked down at the papers in his binder, as if the story would rise from the type there in front of him. "Miss LaBrowne died in a car accident a year after Kasper was born. She had money from a family inheritance and left Kasper a sizable Special Needs Trust, with Gary as Trustee to oversee his care. Your father never had to use your family's resources and, as he requested, we kept all records confidential, with reports mailed to his office. In the early years we used the trust money to pay the bills to a children's care facility, but now Kasper is cared for by Seton Place, a resident health care home for adults in Illinois, one of the best in the country, and the trust pays the bills there. Kasper is twenty-five."

"We have a brother? Kasper is our brother?" said Sophie. She repeated it, as if trying to believe.

Simon leaned toward her again, careful to leave safe space between them. "There's more," he said.

First, I ask that you take responsibility to watch over Kasper and second, I ask that you go to the cabin and, without reading them, burn the notebooks you find there.

Please forgive me. Please try to understand.

Know I love you both. Dad

"Go to the cabin? What cabin!" said Sophie to Cook.

"With money your dad inherited when your grandmother died, he bought a cabin in Estes Park, Colorado where he took Kasper for a week every summer. It's yours now and you must visit there—it's beautiful. I've been many times to Rocky Mountain National Park on birding tours and…"

Sophie interrupted. "Every summer we thought he went on a writing retreat for a week. He said he wanted to write poetry, said his job at the credit union paid the mortgage, but poetry kept his heart beating."

"We weren't allowed to call him," said Simon. "Total immersion he said."

"About Kasper," Cook continued. "Your dad asks that you become joint trustees of the Special Needs Trust, but there should be no concern about the financial side. There's more than enough money left to cover Kasper's lifetime. We are happy to continue to make the payments and interact with the administrators at Seton Place if you don't want any contact with your father's son."

"This is overwhelming," said Simon. "What notebooks at this cabin could be so important to burn before reading?"

"Can't help you there," said Cook, "But we *can* help you navigate the paperwork and the legal side of this transfer of the Trust for your brother."

The unfamiliar words kept repeating in Simon's head. *Your brother. Your brother.*

In the fall a new vaccine was available which targeted the prevalent COVID variants. Sophie and Simon had their shots and felt safe to travel by plane to see the cabin in Estes Park. On the way, anxious about what they would find of their father's that they should burn before reading, they argued.

They argued over what to do next with the house where Dad had lived, where they were raised, their family home, with all the old furniture, his books on raising rabbits, their mother's old jewelry which no one wanted. Sophie wanted to sell the house and take her half of the profit to buy her own place: she was angry at her father. He had ruined their memories in that house, she said. Simon hesitated. He wasn't sure about anything. He delayed signing papers to close bank accounts, transferring title to cars, closing his dad's club memberships—frustrating the paralegal assigned by Cook who was attempting to help him.

They argued over whether to go meet Kasper. They knew, by then, the details about Kasper's cognitive challenges which, though he was in his twenties gave him a mental age estimated at eight; they'd read about his habitual rocking and hand flapping behavior and lack of speech. In the photo Seton Place sent them, his small, oblong-shaped, flat brown face revealed a snub nose, tiny ears, and the tip of a protruding tongue. Sophie saw no family resemblance and the strange face made her uncomfortable. She told Simon she didn't know what they would say to Kasper or what they could do together. Simon wondered if Kasper should be considered for a group home with more stimulation, or moved to a care home near them, or leave him where he was at Seton Place. How would they know if they didn't meet him? Simon argued they had a duty to fulfill Dad's request. Sophie turned to the window. She muttered. "Not that dad. Not anymore."

Once off the plane, they were silent as they drove a rental car into the mountains. They travelled up a winding road past the old Stanley Hotel, continued several miles beyond the Estes Park resort condominiums, to a small brown two-bedroom log cabin, nestled like a bird under the wings of the Needles at Lumpy Ridge.

Inside the cabin, they dropped their backpacks on the floor at the door and looked immediately for their father's papers. In the bookcase next to the fireplace, they found a set of his handwritten notebooks.

Without discussion of their father's wishes, they opened them and began to read.

The notebooks contained their father's poems; they had no idea how to judge the beauty of the writing, but the subject embarrassed them. He wrote openly about sex with their mother. Sophie read only one and, not interested, moved her things into the first bedroom and went to unpack.

Simon took the notebooks to the second bedroom and settled in his bed. When he opened the first journal, his father's familiar cursive with its strong arches and big loops again aroused strong emotions. His anger at his dad and the conflicting love for him flowed over Simon in a wave.

He tried to quiet himself by reading.

...she liked to run her tongue along my inner thigh, brushing her long hair across my body, then wrapping me in her hair...

He felt a softening, a stirring, the long-suppressed ache of desire.

...inside her, I liked to touch her softly on her throat at the spot where medics check for a beating heart.

His father was a man who had loved well. He wasn't perfect, but his life was over. Simon's journey was ahead to create. Whatever his father had done, or not done, had nothing to do with him. Simon felt craving, appetite, hunger to move on.

He asked himself if he would have the courage to grab life, to make tough decisions, to do the right thing with his brother Kasper? Or would he cover it up like his father did, afraid of what people might think?

Their week at the cabin gave them rest and escape, long needed. They discovered the beauty of the turning Aspen trees whispering next to their window at night, the sight of a doe with her fawn in the early morning, the singing of sparrows, warblers, finches, wrens and thrushes throughout the day (they said how delighted Jack Cook would be) and the sweet smell of mountain air washed clean every afternoon by a short thunderstorm.

On their last day, walking to the Stanley to have lunch, they decided to meet Kasper.

It was October, cloudy but unseasonably warm and humid, in Parkville, Illinois. Kasper was sitting on the porch with a man in white, dressed like a nurse. Kasper was so short his feet hung over his chair's cushion, but he easily jumped out of the chair, waving his short stubby arms to greet them. They thought he couldn't speak because of his diminished hearing, but in a loud yell, a strange sound coming from deep in his chest, he jumped up on Simon and said "Dad, Dad." Simon did his best to keep his balance.

The caretaker approached them. "He's been expecting to play his favorite card game, Exploding Kittens. He used to play Go Fish over and over, but his dad got tired of that and introduced this one when it came out a few years ago. Kasper doesn't understand that his father has died and you—it's incredible. You look exactly like Mr. Sims."

Simon hesitated, but only a second, before he wrapped his arms around his brother. No one had touched Simon in this intimate way for a long time. Kasper felt warm, soft, and smelled of lemons. From Simon's arms Kasper noticed Sophie. He held up a sliced lemon wedge he had been sucking, offering it as a gift.

Sophie stepped back, alarmed.

She turned to the caretaker, "But it's been a year; he hasn't seen Dad…and he's confusing Simon with our father."

"Time doesn't seem to register with Kasper," the man said. "It's a blessing."

Sophie disliked people who said *it's a blessing* about things that weren't at all a blessing. "And he's speaking," she said. "We thought he had lost most of his hearing at birth."

"It's the only word he can speak," said the caretaker. "He calls me dad too."

They went inside to a large corner room with a sign on the door that said "Happiness Room." It was full of muted light from windows across the walls of two sides, decorated with yellow fabrics, their shades from gold to pale yellow echoed in sunflowers, roses, dahlias and begonias, all yellow flowers in yellow vases placed about the room. Pulled up to each table were comfortable chairs, some with high seat cushions to accommodate different patient's needs. Kasper climbed up on one of them—clearly it was the chair he was in the habit of claiming. The caretaker brought each of them a glass of water with a fresh lemon slice and a straw. Kasper dropped his old lemon wedge and took the new one in his hand. The caretaker left the three of them sitting in front of cards in a box labeled "Exploding Kittens."

"Exploding Kittens," said Sophie. She took out the rules and read them. "What a silly game, to trick your friends into blowing up."

"Sounds like good fun to me. Look at these creative graphics." Simon said. He read the names of several cards aloud. "Nope, Skip, Diffuse, See the Future. Yep. I'd like to see the future, wouldn't you?"

Kasper laughed as if this was the funniest joke he had ever heard.

Sophie, never good at cards, continued to puzzle over the rules. It didn't matter because Kasper, after he chewed and swallowed his lemon slice, took pleasure in passing out the cards and looking at the graphics on their faces, but he quickly collected them all again and started over with passing them out. As he did this, he rocked back and forth in his chair and periodically pulled his free hand through his hair. He liked the card with the Taco Cat and held on to it, unaware he was crushing it in his hand.

Simon found another Taco Cat card and gave it to Kasper. He received it as if it were Christmas and he'd gotten his favorite present—with a huge smile.

The overcast sky had cleared and sunbeams through the window next to their table warmed Simon's hands. He smelled hot dogs grilling and heard the clinking sounds of people setting silverware on tables in a room nearby. Like a camera, pulling back, his mind saw the scene, trying to normalize it: three adults in their late twenties playing cards around a table. Three siblings, he corrected. One sibling, his half-brother. He looked across at Kasper with his mother's brown skin, his short arms and stubby fingers wrapped around his Taco Cat cards, his almond-shaped eyes, his tightly coiled hair beginning to show premature gray. He looked closely at Kasper's eyes; they were blue. Like his eyes. Like his father's eyes. But Kasper's eyes had the small white spots on the periphery of the iris, typical of Down Syndrome. Staring into his eyes was like looking into a galaxy of a dozen stars, lined in a circle around an indigo sun, his iris.

Kasper paused his movements for a brief moment and looked closely at Simon. Then he began again, rocking, chanting "Dad, Da, Dad," over and over as he continued to pass out cards and then collect them and pass them out again.

Staring at Kasper's eyes, Simon thought about his father—the man who figured out how to automate payments at the credit union, who never forgot his wedding anniversary and consistently brought her favorite blue iris to his mother, who raised rabbits and got excited every time their baby ears would lop—and mourned each bunny when they left for new homes—the same father who hated that his son became a hypnotherapist because he believed hypnosis belonged in a circus sideshow—and didn't hesitate to express his disapproval. This man, this man, this complicated man, unknown to him, had kindly played Go Fish, and Exploding Kittens, with his secret son.

They stood to leave and Kasper changed. His face crumpled into itself and tears fell across his wrinkled cheeks. He jumped up onto Simon again and Simon fell back in his chair with Kasper sideways on his lap, arms around his neck, sobbing.

In the car, after they left, Sophie said she wondered how Dad ever managed to travel with Kasper with his special needs or take care of him at the cabin for a week. "I could never manage Kasper's care. I bet he took a caretaker from the home to help," said Sophie.

Simon regretted having to leave Kasper so upset. "He did think I was Dad after all," he murmured to himself.

On the return trip to California—to home, with all its pending decisions and the challenge of next steps—Simon tried to think of possibilities. What if the pandemic were definitely over and he could forget about COVID, forget about using Zoom which he hated? What if he gave his condo to Sophie and moved into his father's house? What if he used Dad's front office with its private entry to the garden as a place to meet his patients? What if he brought Kasper to live in the downstairs wing? What if he used Kasper's trust money to pay a live-in nurse for his daily care instead of giving it to Seton

Place? He imagined Kasper's joy playing with his first Holland Lop bunny. Wouldn't he be happier?

As the plane neared the San Francisco airport, Simon looked out his window at the variegated quilt of the salt ponds, their faded fuchsias, oranges, and reds turning to blues and greens, as the salt making slowly gave way to restored marsh. As the plane landed, he reached up and touched his throat at the spot where medics check for a beating heart. He felt the blood pulsing under his finger.

#theprocedure

My fingers drum the keypad, as rhythmic as her heartbeat. Although forty years have passed, I remember the wet, earthy scent of her newborn hair.

You are imagining, says Dr. Beam.

The three bars for the clinic's Wi-Fi on my iPad flicker to two, threatening a weak signal, but then the Twitter app loads fine. Learning Twitter as a form of therapy is recommended by Dr. Beam, head of palliative care.

She walks in my mind, I say. She has a birthday.

You can only grieve so long, he says, before it demands release, like a woman holding in a scream.

Forty years. Might be long enough to hold in a scream.

I'm keeping my handle secret, but the hashtags I chose were #theprocedure, with an optional #choice, rejecting the use of straight-out #abortion, which might turn off followers at this early stage. I'd never gone public before.

The white screen light washes over me like a cleansing. The secrecy protects me, safe as a church confessional. In the profile, I never use my real name.

Through Twitter I meet @TwinkleLittleStar and @OldFartHead. @Twinkle tweets that having #theprocedure with a pill has fewer side effects than the old fashioned #D&Csurgical-abortion method which, in the past, had been known to cause depression. This reminds @OldFart that when weapons were guns, and a soldier could see the man he shot, a life for a life meant something, but now that we use drones, war has minimal side effects too.

People make strange connections online says Dr. Beam when I tell him later. I say they make strange connections in person too. Nothing new there.

@Twinkle taught me that you can add a photograph. @Fart said Tweets with a picture have more engagement rates. @Twinkle is pregnant, considering #theprocedure. She already has five children. @Fart says he is certain he never got a girl pregnant. Sadly, he could not even get his own wife pregnant. After a week together online, those two are my best friends.

Dr. Beam says it is misleading to attach a photo of a baby girl.

When radiation makes me feel better temporarily, it is Dr. Beam's idea for me to volunteer at the clinic. On the first day I meet Trisha. Everyone has to have counseling before they make *the decision*. Dr. Beam says I would have benefitted from counseling too. I said, it would have been a good idea, if they had counseling back then, but considering my procedure was illegal, they could hardly offer counseling, could they?

Trisha's boyfriend just graduated from law school and, although she loves him, and they plan to marry, until he gets a job, she says now is not a good time to be pregnant. She asks if I ever had children, you know, afterwards.

I say eventually I had two wonderful boys, grown up now.

She mentions something about a daughter. She wants a girl when the time is right.

The word, *daughter,* echoes a bit, like in a tunnel when the scream lingers.

But I told Trisha what she wanted to hear: that I had no regrets. No regrets at all.

I had a very bad stomach cramp right then, had to go home.

Dr. Beam frowns when I tell him. He says the clinic is not like Twitter. He says even the President lies on Twitter.

The President lies in person too I say.

But you're not the President are you.

Dr. Beam is a master at stating the obvious.

After the relapse, I give up the clinic in favor of more time to Tweet. I tell Dr. Beam that my mind moves toward peace one Tweet at a time. Breakfast, lunch, dinner, evening instead of television, before and after treatments, everything framed by Twitter. My husband, a patient man, responds to my addiction by asking to learn to Tweet, but he still can't manage a simple tag on Facebook.

He doesn't know about her.

Dr. Beam says sharing hobbies can be useful, but what we really need is to talk about IT. About her. About how she died.

I still think of her as living. I rub her feet after she runs her first marathon, I serve her pints of salted caramel ice cream when she is nervous about exams, I settle her head on my shoulder to cry over the first boyfriend's betrayal.

As I lay dying, she will hold my hand. She will refuse to let me go.

Big Lies

My first husband abandoned me for a childhood friend. He began leaving me alone during the hot Chicago evenings, going for walks he said. When fall's blustery winds began, there were whole nights he did not return. After work, afraid to go back to our lonely room, I walked downtown by the river. Sometimes I stopped to look down into the black water, tempted, but I could hear my dead father's voice above the wind. Dad never approved of suicide for any reason.

My husband was a young nineteen and I, almost twenty-one. It was late 1969 and the government had escalated the undeclared war in Vietnam with the first draft lottery since the Korean War in 1950. As I look back on my younger self, some fifty years later, I think about the other wars that followed: the Persian Gulf War, the War in Afghanistan, the War in Iraq, the Syrian Civil War, the Libyan Civil War, the War on Terror. I can't remember all of them. Vietnam was only the beginning.

My young husband and I were injured with wounds from our past. Mine was the death of my father in a car accident. If only I had taken time to return Dad's kiss that last time I saw him. My husband was estranged from his parents for reasons he would not explain. He did not miss his dad, but sometimes at night in his dreams, he cried out for his mother. We had dropped out of college, against the advice of our families, to get married. He was looking for a job; I worked for a typing service. We lived in a closet-size rented room with a shared bath down the fetid hallway, eating on the floor and sleeping on a mattress we found left on the street. Outside our one window, the Chicago elevated train shook our building every time it screamed by.

In addition to ten one-quart canteens of water, food ration, an air mattress, a poncho, and an extra pair of socks, an infantryman in Vietnam carried a rifle or machine gun, ammunition in a full magazine or bandolier, and a supply of hand grenades, *on his back*.

34

The average rucksack weight was eighty-five pounds. The guilt and grief we carried from our young secrets weighed more. Like soldiers, we carried our guilt in extreme humidity, through knee-deep mud, and up bug-infested hilltops through the jungle of our marriage when, like a bomb, the draft papers arrived.

Certain deferments were available: College men, for example, or married men with children.

A few days after he got the draft papers, an unmarried woman at work found me crying in the restroom. Unhappy herself, she confessed to being pregnant with a child she did not want. She had hooded eyes, like those of my love. It made it easier to ask her. After she agreed, she said "This baby might as well be good for something."

I still hear her saying this.

Home pregnancy tests purchased at the drugstore were unheard of then. I went to a clinic. I carried this kind stranger's pregnant urine in a Mason jar with a screw-on lid which I had bought at the Goodwill. It leaked in my purse leaving a strong ammonia smell on my cloth wallet, on my handkerchief, on my makeup bag. I poured what remained into the specimen cup in the secrecy of the clinic's bathroom.

Sitting in that clinic, presenting my faked sample, I worried that they would notice my hands shaking. I worried my guilt would show in my frightened face. I worried that somehow they could tell it wasn't my child in that fluid. I worried that even if the government didn't find out my lie, my dead father would know. *God would know.*

Even after I washed my hands, I smelled her urine on my fingers. Afterwards, I ran all the way to the bus stop. When I got home, I threw away the purse and all its contents.

It was not a war protest as I pretended. It was a last cry for his love.

He did not die in Vietnam. Proof of his impending fatherhood gave him a pass and he was not drafted. We never had children. He left me for his best friend from childhood, a man whose name I cannot say. After the divorce, I never saw him again. He might have died from AIDS in the 1980s.

I should not have been concerned about my wartime lie: A film about the Vietnam War streaming on PBS claims that the President, the military leaders, and the Vietnamese all lied to us.

Part II: Sins and Regrets

Cool Shirt

His car hits the wall, flips over and bursts into flames. I think about his oily eyes, his lubricating fingers, his vanity biceps crisping up like burned bacon while everyone in the grandstands watches.

His flame-resistant driver's fire suit works only long enough for him to know he's going to die.

From the paddock, with the crew wives, *she* watches. I think about his cruel mouth as he told me, laughed about her little squeals, like a pup, he said, as she came. She's *my* wife—I know about the squeals.

I think about the seconds before the crash when the temperature inside the car reached one hundred forty degrees. I think about the blood racing to cool his skin, deserting his brain. I think about the heat, his tingling hands and toes, his dizziness, his blurred vision, then his inability to steer.

Or earlier, before the race, when he stepped into the cockpit of his car and plugged in his cool shirt, feeling the cold water ripple over him through the coiling capillary tubing, winding and twisting like so many blue veins outside his body, as refreshing as jumping in a mountain lake.

I think about his panic when he stopped feeling it as I knew he would.

I don't think about the day he won Le Mans, how we stood on the podium together, lead driver and me, his trusted crew chief, how he raised his arms with his fingers flexed around the trophy blazing in the sun.

Caught in Headlights

I am the second Mrs. Roberts. Lily, with her long blonde hair, bushy as dried wheat stalks, with her doe-eyes, indigo with black at the edges, with her way of crossing those long leaping legs and leaning toward me to talk, as if I were the only person she had ever loved— Lily. She was Hector's first. His first wife.

She died.

I cannot bear to say how it happened. Not yet. Though I see you want to know, your impatient foot tapping on the floor that way. I'm giving you three sessions. That's all. I'm final about that.

I hear the water tinkling from the fountain in your waiting room. Silence rolls between us like a bus passing.

We are a threesome in our marriage now. Hector, me, and Lily's ghost. In our bed, feeling his unshaved chin rub my cheek, prickling raw like gritty sandpaper, while I'm counting backwards from one hundred until he finishes, I smell her. She is chocolate melting, warm cat fur, fun trashy makeup, strawberry flavored nail polish, hair spray, sweat. My mind goes to the first time we met at her salon. While he groans, I imagine her gentle fingers on my scalp as she wraps my hair in foil for my highlights. Her touch so respectful, no pulling, as she layers my fine strands. So different from the way he grabs my hair in his fist, forgetting not to hurt me as he thrusts and thrusts.

I've never confessed this to anyone. I feel the giveaway red line of blush working its way up my cheeks.

You lean forward, threads of hair dripping down over your left eye.

We lock in a stare like two bucks with our antlers braided together.

You remind me of my father, his shock of unruly red hair, bronze mustache, broad forehead, his long nose. I used to joke that his main purpose in life was to get me to confess. He could outstare me longer than you can. His gaze, like the threat of capture from a hunter's net gun, made me tell him whatever it was he expected. I lied often.

You win. I have to look away first. When I look down, I see the toe of my scuffed Dansko Nursing Clogs, once shiny, now bruised, droplets of blood spatter dried on the surface.

"Dolores," you say. "Where were you when Lily died?"

I don't remember. (I lie.)

I do remember late August 2020. I see the sky flooded with burnt orange, from the smoke of a hundred wildfires—the largest wildfire season in California's history. People were caged in their houses under the suffocated sunlight. As if COVID wasn't enough to end the world as we knew it.

Lily had to give birth in the hallway; all the hospital beds were taken by COVID patients.

There is a long silence while I seek to bring the details into focus. I see the baby, covered in the vernix, slippery, hard to hold as a child's toy water wiggle. It's a boy. I've spotted a tiny penis in the mess. His fawn eyes have black at the edges, like hers, but his skin is dark, like Hector's.

I listen for his cry.

I see a bright light and I am stunned, caught like a deer in headlights.

Here we are again. Another patient was waiting when I came in and I feel pressured to hurry, get this over with.

Did I say I am the second Mrs. Roberts?

Hector says I'm as annoying as the character in the movie Groundhog Day, repeating the same thing over and over.

Did I tell you that Lily was my hair stylist—and one day at my highlights appointment—her husband came by to see her. That's how I met Hector. He's handsome, makes her laugh, but he sometimes drinks too much, has a temper. She's never been lucky picking men.

Lily died suddenly in a violent way and he was crushed to lose her. Turned to me for sympathy and one thing led to another. I confess I loved her too. All those times I sat in her salon chair, with her standing over me, hands on my hair. My eyes at breast level, I stared at her soft, well-rounded arms, at the jade bracelet she wore every day, and I smelled the citrus-fresh scented hair mist on her apron, so close to my face.

When Hector's baby was growing in her womb and her breasts threatened to burst out of the apron, it was all I could do sitting there under her clipping scissors to resist touching her. Once I moved my head close and my lips brushed the tip of her nipple, enlarged behind the apron.

I feel my face warm; the giveaway red line of my blush is working its way up my cheeks. As you lean forward a shock of red hair falls over one eye.

I like to imagine being a hair stylist like Lily—understanding how to use all those shears, clippers, trimmers, razors, combs, and brushes, the blow dryer, the black capes—and always a clean towel at her washing station. Sometimes I would compare the list of our professional tools: my stethoscope, thermometer, tongue depressor, bandages, pen, and clip board. I dream of her touching me under my nursing lab coat.

"Did she touch you?" You stare at me, locking your weapon eyes onto mine.

You win. I look away because I don't want to say it was Hector who touched me. He changed during her pregnancy, always bumping up against me when the three of us got together, putting his hand on my leg under the table, his groping fingers where they shouldn't be. I look down at my clogs and see a fly perched on the blood-spattered toe. I shake my foot. As it flies away, I hear the buzzing over the top of the tinkling fountain in your lobby.

Once Lily gave me jewel shoe charms, thinking I wore Crocs to work. I save them still in a box on my vanity.

I am not a regular Labor and Delivery nurse. I'm a float nurse, stuck in the float pool. L&D belongs to the experts on the maternity ward. That day, when they brought her in, and there were no rooms, and she was frightened of catching COVID (it was before the vaccines), she asked for me. They called me on the paging system.

She did not die at childbirth. She was fine. The baby was fine. Hector came after the birth to take her home, but he refused to hold his newborn. They had a fight—I don't know about what. I came down to Maternity from the Advanced Treatment Center, after my shift was over, to say goodbye to them. Immediately I understood he had been drinking; you could smell the stink of whisky off his angry breath. I should have offered to drive.

"Dolores," you say. "The police report says you *were* driving."

I am silent for a long while, trying to focus on the details.

I see the baby lying in the road after an accident, his body, bloody, his tiny penis shaken out of his newborn diaper, his fawn eyes with the dark at the edges.

I listen for his cry.

I blink from the bright light. I am frozen, like a doe startled at night by a car on the road.

Today I've worn my new Crocs; I put the jewel charms Lily gave me into the holes. To bring me luck. I'm determined this will be my last session.

I am the second Mrs. Roberts. Have I mentioned that?

Lily was buried on a stormy Sunday, in sheets of rain. Sunday, appropriate for her. Always a day of rest for hair stylists whose feet swell from a week of standing. A nurse rarely sits on the job either. It's why I wear the clogs; they provide support for long hours on my feet.

I longed to see her again—to caress her long blonde hair, to press my lips to her indigo eyes, closed in death. But Hector demanded a closed casket, said she wasn't presentable after the accident. As the coffin was lowered into the ground, he held my hand in his rigid grasp, dressed against the rain in a coat the shade of stone.

"Dolores," you say. "What about the baby?"

I can't answer.

Silence rolls between us again, heavy as a bus passing.

Without her, I was lost. Hector and I married as soon as we recovered from our injuries. I thought being married to him would bring her back to me. There was some confusion with the accident and he said it was better if we were married so we couldn't testify against each other. He promised to give up drinking.

You lean forward, your hair dripping across your face, just like my old dad. Our eyes lock in the stare-down you use to force me to confess.

You win. I look away first, down at my shoes. I see the Crocs with her shoe charms. I feel Lily in the room with me.

I should have been driving. I always drove when Hector was drinking and the three of us were together. Lily didn't drive; she had an anxiety disorder and the stress of driving made it worse.

"Dolores," you say. "The police report says you *were* driving."

A long silence unfolds like a blanket while I seek to bring the details into focus.

That's not true. Hector told the police that I was driving so he could avoid another DUI. That night, in the hospital parking lot, he shoved me aside, slammed me into the back seat next to the baby in his infant car seat. Fearing Hector's temper, I did not object.

I hate myself for this weakness.

I feel your warm hand on my shoulder. You hand me a tissue for my tears.

Minutes before the accident the baby is screaming, fighting his car seat harness. To comfort him, I do the unthinkable thing. I unhook his safety straps and lift him onto my lap. As I hold the baby in my arms, I feel his small hand in mine, his tiny, bewitching fingers wrapped around my thumb. It's the palmar grasp reflex, common in newborns.

Then the bright light—and a loud crash.

The oncoming car hit toward the passenger side—I see Lily's lifeless hand on the pavement next to me where we were both thrown. I look for the baby. I see his new toys—his soft sleepy bear, a pacifier, one slipper sock—among the broken glass.

I listen for his cry.

Sin of Omission

At the checkout when the old man next in line forgets his wallet, Max keeps on bagging his own groceries: three boxes of Nature's Path Corn Flakes, twelve packages of peanut M&Ms, three bags of Kettle potato chips, organic with sea salt, a bunch of bananas, almond milk. He feels the curve of a banana against his palm as he hears the teenage clerk and the old man in conversation. The old man says how easy it is these days to forget his wallet when he has to remember the mask, and the house keys, and to bring his own bags. Once he forgot to change into his outdoor shoes, went out in his slippers, he says, laughing.

Later Max tells himself he was distracted by the din of people in line arguing about the latest COVID guidelines, the tempting smell of grinding coffee beans from the coffee station in the corner, the commotion over at the Amazon return station when the clerk couldn't read someone's QR code on their phone. He was not thinking about the old man; he was thinking about himself, how he should buy more vegetables. Since the Pandemic he's overloaded on candy, had cereal for dinner, chips afterwards, while streaming old TV shows. Some mornings, he's surprised to wake up on the couch.

The old man continues the conversation as if he is chatting with a friend, extending the time he stands there, while the clerk explains she can't do anything. No, she can't hold the groceries for later pickup. It's the rules. Her boss would fire her. Her young voice has a tone—apathy, indifference, boredom. The old man won't stop chatting; it's harder since my grandson came to live with me, he says.

Max hadn't seen the child until then. A small, doe-eyed boy, barely tall enough to see over the counter, stares hungrily at Max's M&Ms. The boy's Star Wars shirt has a big hole in the shoulder and he nervously pulls at the frayed cloth. As Max picks up his two bags, hearing a crunch sound and angry at himself for absent mindedly putting the chips under the milk carton, he smells something sour coming from the old man. Second-hand clothes, unwashed for a while?

On the drive home he mentally beats himself up. Why didn't he offer to pay for the old man's groceries? He could have. Easily. Why didn't he at least give the child a package of his M&Ms? Why wasn't he *that* man?

When he gets home, unpacking the candy, he sees the eyes of the boy. He sees the eyes of the boy when he turns on his big screen TV. He sees the eyes of the boy when he tries to sleep. Five years later, in the hospital for surgery, counting backwards before the anesthetic kicks in, thinking about his life, he will see the boy's begging eyes.

A Conversation Between Two Sisters
with a Hawk Watching

"What should we do with the body?"

*Chased by two black crows, the young hawk has dropped his murdered
mouse on the grass in the corner of their afternoon. But Sister doesn't mean that
body.*

"Cover your old, wrinkled skin with red chiffon. Drape scarlet
scarves up to your ear lobes."
"What's wrong with my ear lobes?"
"Don't be snappy. I'm trying to help."
"*Your* neck is the one needs covering, your shaky wattles."
"Elephant ears."
"Turkey neck."
"Let's not squabble."

*The unpracticed hawk perches in the redwood tree, watching. Behind the
hawk's turned head, the sun sets scarlet.*

"Once I was the lovely younger daughter, the one with thick
curly hair, who loved to rip off my rags, run wild."
"You *still are* the beautiful one. I'm forever the older, smarter
sister."
"Beautiful? Not me. I've collected six degenerative discs, a dead
rotator cuff, shaky knees, and stomach sag,"
"How did we get so old?"
"My ultimate humiliation—going bald."
"Hard to believe what life does to hair."

*A feather drops as he settles his wings, plumage thick from his second
molting. Sister will find it in the morning.*

"Once we were hot."

"We could wrap men around our little fingers."

"Our skin was peaches and cream."

"We were never getting old."

"Not like our mother."

"We were never going to be our mother."

"I have her aged hands. The palm bump, the bent finger."

"Mom's clichés fill my mouth when I'm not looking."

Across the darkening grass, the seemingly murdered mouse moves.

"Once we had children."

"Babies at our breasts became boys with smelly shoes, grew into adult sons who have boys with smelly shoes."

"Back in our day husbands managed our lives as if we were kittens."

"Their little pets, in patriarchy."

"We loved them, we held them when they cried, we watched them pass."

"We let them go."

"We let them go."

The mouse scampers across the shadows. Not his turn. Not this time.

"What should we do with the body?"

"You asked that already."

"Short term memory, shot to hell."

"Bury my old body, dirt, graveyards, tomb stones…candles burning in church."

"Not me. Cremation. Burn this old thing."

"Drama Queen—going up in flames."

"I confess. I always wanted scarlet hair."

"Dye it red. Dare you. It's never too late—*as long as we're breathing.*"

The last five words perch like the hawk in the tree, waiting…

"Let's go inside. You wash the kale."
"I'll start the rice cooking."
"Here, take my hand. I'll push open the screen door, help you over the threshold."
"Thank you. At least your knees aren't gone."
"Please don't die."
"Please don't die *first.*"

The hawk's wings disappear into darkness, but he remains present in the tree, his yellow eyes open, glowing like flashlights.

Toccata and Fugue

At the coffee shop where he took me afterwards, he played the Bach Toccata and Fugue in D minor on the inside of my lower arm, tapping a few notes, raising my blond hairs, tickling my skin. He leaned forward across the table, whispered the Kimball Organ measurements in my ear, *4 manuals, 96 speaking stops, 96 ranks, 5,949 pipes*. I felt the beat all the way to my toes, everything pulsing. Right away he took liberties, called me Hella, his shining light, though I preferred Helena. He was Noland, Nollie for short, he said. Because he had a class after the coffee, I walked back to the dorm alone, singing *Nollie, Nollie, Nollie*, rolling the word on my tongue like the toccata, developing full chords and rapid runs in my head. Already I was in love.

I met him for the first time an hour before in the empty cathedral; he sat on the bench of the Kimball Organ, lightly fingering the keys. It was a quiet Wednesday afternoon with no one else present. The cathedral held its silence, a silence thick with past choirs, hymns, recitals, a whispered Lord's Prayer. Cushioned benches, folded back kneelers, the weekly bulletin, Bibles and hymnals peeking out of pockets on the back of pews, were speckled in the light from stained glass windows. The shadows from the colored glass cut patterns on the center aisle's red carpet, like leaves of trees shadowed on a forest floor. The air, close and cool, smelled of history, of perfumed robes, of freshly washed children, of lilies carefully arranged by the altar women, a hundred years of devoted service.

I was not religious, did not attend the Anglican services. An introvert, the quiet cathedral was my favorite place for relief from sharing a dorm room, for respite from the huge lecture halls packed with long-haired boys and girls in tie-dyed shirts and frayed jeans, for escape from the noise of city traffic and crowded college paths, a rare place to be alone. The magic of the cathedral, the thrill of secretly feeling the organ's keys, as Nollie encouraged me to pretend-play, the air, the light, the echoes of past music became part of him, of my memory of him, our meeting, our first love.

My young self was tall, thin, with boyish legs and slim chest, hazel-green eyes, light brown, shoulder-length hair. I was good at my studies, a journalism major, dreaming of revealing truth in investigative articles for the New York Times, the Washington Post. But socially, I was obsessed with my failure to match up to the curves of the popular girls, or to find my type in the photos of women in magazines, or to fit the current fashion in clothes. I remained, at nineteen, completely unaware of my beauty. A virgin. Possibly the only virgin left on campus. Humiliated by this fact. Embarrassed to discuss it.

Noland was dark skinned, lefthanded, had the slender, long fingers of a pianist. His dark brown hooded eyes made me think of intrigue, mystery, bedrooms. A music major, he laughingly confessed to an addiction, not to weed, but to Bach. We spent hours listening to Bach's famous organ works—the Toccata and Fugue in D minor, the Passacaglia and Fugue in C minor, or the Fugue in G minor, which were easy for him to play. Holding hands together in silence, both loving patterns, loving the triumphant moment when a piece of music returned to the tonic, or the fugue surprised by presenting harmony with a slowed down version of itself.

Raised on fairy tales of Prince Charming and myths of living a happily-ever-after marriage, with lack of physical intimacy replaced by the intensity of music, I imagined that he was *the one*. He was so handsome he drew stares when we walked together, and some day he was going to be a famous composer, and we shared the love of music—the perfect man I thought. Now when I look back on this time, I understand how unaware I was, unaware of Nollie as a person, unaware of *his* motives.

I recognize that the young Hella had difficulty making decisions, even where to go to dinner, or what movie, or whether—with Nollie—when his kissing went on so long—to push having sex. We dated for a year full of what I came to think of as his unbearable kissing, with each passionate touch ending up in the air, like a misplaced gap in the musical notation, a place where the notes were meant to rise instead of rest, but the composer had a break in thought, or a headache, or was interrupted by his children wanting to play.

When his high school friend David came to visit, something happened to Nollie. Suddenly Nollie urged marriage, as if that decision, that formal commitment, was needed to allow him, as he said, to go *all the way*. I felt his desperation, the pushing, the hurried asking, as if tomorrow would be too late, but I did not listen to my heart, I did not like to ask what was wrong. When he asked me to marry him, I said *yes* immediately, before really thinking, before understanding *my* motives.

It came that night, that welcome ending of my virginity. Nollie was in his junior year, had his own one-room apartment. David was out visiting his cousins, to say good- bye one last time before he left for Vietnam. Nollie had given David his front door key to use on return. His long pianist-fingers lingered too long in David's palm as he laid the key in his hand. I felt the spark between them like a punch in my gut, but I did not examine it. After David left, Nollie took me in his arms for his unbearable kissing and I pushed the image away.

Bach's Toccata and Fugue pounded, for the hundredth time, on the expensive stereo system which Nollie had bought with his parents' money instead of furniture. In the dark scary corner where the thin mattress he found abandoned in the hallway lay on the floor, the intense touch of his long fingers on my neck, the scrape of the hard floor through the thin mattress as he pushed against me, the smoky scent of dinner on his hot skin, were quickly forgotten. What I remembered, during the sudden silence when the music ended, was anxiously listening for the sound of David's key turning in the lock.

Noland was my first husband. We were married for two years. Before it ended, he left me over and over for others whose names I never knew. To afford to marry, I had dropped out of school, got a job in a typing pool, pressing meaningless words of others onto the page. In those years I got used to waiting, to listening for his feet climbing the stairs, to seeking solace in libraries, in crowds on the street, in books. Alone for nights at a time, ashamed that I was unworthy of love, I walked by the river and looked down into its green depths, or stood above the tracks of the commuter train, head bowed. During sleepless nights, I imagined pill containers emptied, bloodied wrists, my neck broken in a leap from the window ledge. One night, and the next night, and the next, I waited, life frozen in place. One day I came home, and his stereo system was gone. He had moved out. He left me a one-line note saying he was sorry he was gay.

I told myself I should have known he was a deceiver from his hooded eyes, those brown eyes shaded with lashes drawn down like half-mast flags, hiding, never looking directly at me. When he left me, and I threw away his photographs, I realized in every picture he looked away from me, at the sky, or some far away spot at the top of a tree, or upwards as if at a passing bird.

I was furious, blamed him, claimed *he* should be ashamed, deceiving me, using me. Later, after time passed and the anger diminished, I told myself our marriage failed because I was so young. And there was always music playing. I confused love of the music with love of the man. Feeling his fugues were complicit, I could no longer listen to Bach.

Through years in my twenties, I dated unsuccessfully, floundered at jobs, moved cities, as if a new location could cure my problem. At thirty, one night in a dream my subconscious brought back the night on the mattress in Nollie's apartment. Instead of passion, I recognized a feeling of pride, pride in finding the dark ripe blood of the ruptured hymen on my fingers, in leaving it for proof of our loving on Nollie's mattress. In the dream I announced my loss of virginity to my dorm friends the next day, as if it were a badge of honor, instead of a moment of joy. I woke, smelling blood, drenched in shame. I understood I had used Nollie, had used marriage, as he had used marriage—to meet the world's expectations, not for love.

In the morning, I turned to Bach again. Sleepers Awake. Air on a G String. The Toccata and Fugue in D minor. Now it was mine, this music; I did not need a man to confirm my worth. My worth belonged to me. It was my responsibility.

At this moment, when the present overlays my view of the past, and I bring to that night, to Hella and Nollie, a mature woman's wisdom, I can finally understand the struggle going on in young Nollie. It should have been obvious in the stares of other men, in the way he asked me to touch him, in his hesitations. He loved someone else. He loved David, but he thought David was forbidden to him. He made love to Hella, but it was David in his mind that night. It was David he touched with his long fingers, David he entered on the mattress on the floor.

On a visit to my old college, I return to the Anglican cathedral to view the Kimball Organ, recently restored. I settle back on the cushioned pew, facing the chancel and the Kimball's shiny silver pipe façade, thirty-two feet in height. Silence washes over me like a warm bath, light fills my body, cloistered air wraps around me like an embrace. I see Nollie's long fingers, hear his laugh when he says he is addicted to Bach, wonder, as I have many times, if the beautiful boy died of AIDS. Unexpected music speaks from the organ, a student I surmise, here to practice. I do not recognize these modern notes, but I let myself be taken by the music, taken back, taken forward, seduced.

Part III: Secret Desires

Parallel Octaves

Lena was raised on violin lessons and minimal parental supervision. Maestro Ludwig, her first violin teacher, was spiritually her only family. After early morning lessons, before she went off to school, they liked to relax together on the cool sheets of his unmade bed in his private studio in the Hyatt Regency, her violin lying between them. They smelled plumeria and coconut-scented sunscreen lotion from Kaanapali Beach through the one open window.

Maestro, who was twenty years older than Lena, knew her young body better than anyone—her left-hand fingers with callouses from the expensive gold-series Pirastro string set he bought for her, her neck with the dark red chin-rest mark under her left jaw, how her newly developed breasts shuddered when she attempted the highest note, the shrill, ear-piercing A-7. Yet he had acted toward her only as a teacher should. He occasionally hugged her, but it was the way she imagined a father who loved her would hug.

Lena's unhappy parents had lived together in the Presidential Suite on the top floor of the Hyatt Regency until they divorced, and her mother moved back to the mainland. A spacious living room decorated with wicker furniture, popular in the 1980s, a large master bedroom with a king size bed, and a den with a pull-out sofa bed made up the two thousand square foot suite she knew as her childhood home. Her father was busy, constantly gone on trips. Lena had slept on the pull-out sofa bed for as long as she could remember, grew up on snacks from room service, and was used to sand, from tourists' beach walks, tickling her bare feet in the elevator as she played around the hotel, watched out for by the maids.

"Time for the daily feeding," Maestro said, up on his elbow, looking across the violin between them. In addition to teaching private lessons, he worked as penguin habitat manager for the Regency which provided room and board. The daily penguin feeding on view in the atrium lobby for hotel patrons and visitors, was scheduled every morning at 9:30 a.m. The African black-footed penguin was originally from the Cape of Good Hope, but the hotel penguins were born in Ohio.

"Just like me, my family was originally from Samoa, but I was born in Honolulu," Maestro said, smiling, comparing himself to his penguins once, when she was much younger and easily impressed.

When Lena started her lessons, due to the lack of attention at home, she was a repressed seven-year-old with extreme shyness, afraid to fail, afraid even to lift her bow to the strings. She was like the instrument, Maestro said, hollow inside to allow sound to vibrate within. He explained it was his job to let the music into her heart, to help her soul vibrate. No matter what he said, in the beginning Lena could not play. Finally, in one desperate moment, he pointed out how, just as the violin must emerge from its rigid fiberglass case, in the same way, she might, if she wanted, emerge from her clothes. Lena slowly took off her dress, leaving on her girlish panties covered with flamingoes, picked up her violin and began to play. In some strange subconscious way, like swimming in the ocean, she felt free without her clothes.

Until she was eleven, Lena undressed before each lesson, but once her breasts developed, she began to be embarrassed in her underwear and slipped on a silk robe. She had been in love with Maestro for as long as she could remember. By eleven, in everything she played, her vibrato pulsed with the tremulous effect the Maestro's nearness had on her, her wrist shaking, finger moving below pitch and back, as if landing on pitch became the yearning she felt to kiss, to touch, to hold her teacher as close as she held her violin. He did not guess she had a crush on him and she did not confess. After each lesson she dressed, folded the robe carefully and packed it inside the top of her violin case.

She first heard the Paganini Caprice Number 24 on a record, an ancient Itzhak Perlman recording which Maestro played. This was her goal, to play this piece, with its parallel octaves, extremely fast scales and arpeggios, high finger positions, left-hand pizzicato, complex trills, and quick string crossings. Maestro said she had to practice and practice and practice, learning each technique so well that when she played, the music came as if it flowed from her body. He called it "being in the zone" like a sports player. At night in bed, she practiced parallel octaves, tracing invisible notes up and down her sheets.

"Moana keeps trying to be my new mother," Lena said, touching her violin on the bed next to her, absently rubbing the skin of the tailpiece. Her dad had a new wife, Moana. She had moved into the Penthouse Suite with her dad and Lena. "She wants to meet you. My father says he never met you since my mother hired you."

Lena had suspected, for a long time, that Maestro Ludwig was not his real name. He was different from the few other men she knew, her wealthy Jewish father whose business as "investments advisor" was a mystery to her, her two male teachers at the private girls' school who were old men, their bodies hidden in suits. Compared to them, Maestro was young, wore shorts and unbuttoned floral-patterned Aloha shirts which revealed well-developed pectoral muscles and a brief view of his nipples. He had dark curly hair and a gentle, soft, Islander accent. On a desk he had a pile of business cards which had the words "First Chair Coaching" and "Orchestrates Success." Once a year he took a month off from lessons and his penguins when his sister was home from her job as a housekeeper on a Princess Cruise ship. In Lena's life, this had always been the longest, most lonely month of the year.

"Suggest a dinner in the Swan Court," he said. "I'll wear a suit. Perhaps she'll like me then."

But the dinner was cancelled. Moana discovered the silk robe inside Lena's violin case. Despite Lena's arguments that "nothing had happened," Moana convinced Lena's father to fire Maestro. Moana said a hotel penguin habitat manager was not qualified to call himself a violin teacher. Lena was puzzled at the strange prejudice Moana, who was an Islander, seemed to have against other Islanders.

When Lena and Maestro said goodbye, he hugged her for the last time. It was the old Maestro hug, the way she imagined a father who loved her would hug. Lena never saw the Maestro again. She was immediately enrolled in a private school on the mainland and sent to live with her mother. A few years later, she was accepted at the University of Southern California Thornton School of Music and she moved to Los Angeles.

In January of 2020, when Lena was forty-seven, she was appointed the first woman music director of the Boston Symphony Orchestra, one of only six women in the United States who headed symphony orchestras. Three months later COVID closed hotels, shuttered the symphony halls, and prohibited in-person lessons. She had never married and lived alone, forced to shelter in place by herself. For months the only intimacy, the only touch she experienced, the only sound of another voice in the empty rooms of her house, except for Zoom calls, was her violin, vibrating.

After early morning practice she and her violin liked to relax together on the cool sheets of her unmade bed, the old remembered scents of plumeria and coconut on her mind. Once, when she felt scared and lonely, she thought of the Maestro's sister, wondering if she was still on a cruise ship, quarantined for months because Hawaii wouldn't let her ship dock. But she might be dead, the Maestro too.

"Lena-light, moon-light, sunlight," she heard Maestro's voice, chanting her name in his deep voice, sweet as a cello. How did he learn the violin? How did he learn to feed penguins? She never asked him about his training, about his education, his background, about his life. Did she dream Maestro and his lessons? Did she make him up, like a child's imaginary friend?

During the worst moments of isolation, when she felt like screaming, instead she turned to her instrument and played the highest note, the shrill, ear-piercing A-7. Afterwards, relieved, she cuddled her violin like a lover, spooning. She was the big spoon, cocooning the violin's smaller body in a sideways hug, her chest to its back, her breasts, remembering.

Echo of Exploding Bombs

Anna danced the first dance with Morris at her sister's wedding party the evening before the groom, a USAAF pilot, was scheduled to leave for France to bomb the Germans at Saint-Malo. She was eighteen and guessed Morris was older, perhaps a mature twenty-five. Morris touched her naked arm with light magic fingers as he asked her to dance. He added would she mind that he was blind?

The smells of pound cake and garden flowers, the chatter of the old aunts sitting in chairs by the wall, the rustling of her sister Mary's long lace dress as it brushed the floor to the waltz rhythm from the gramophone, filled her mind and prevented her from understanding at first.

He repeated himself, stammering.

So many were blind, or lost limbs, or came home to Chicago half-crazy that summer of 1944 that Anna was not surprised. Gus, the rude best man, good friends with the groom since childhood, was a Navy man, who had lost his arm at Pearl Harbor. Mary asked her to make allowances for his bad behavior. Many of the newly crippled men shrank back ashamed, or like Gus, grew unpleasant.

She longed to run her fingers across his face, but instead she traced down his arm and reached for his hand. As she squeezed it, she felt the cold, shaking tremors of his shyness, smelled the freshly washed shirt and the Brylcreem on his hair, and heard his boots shuffle nervously against the wood flooring. His breath in her ear made strange sounds. Perhaps he was counting steps? When they danced, he kept one hand out behind her, waving it in the empty air, and she understood he was new to blindness.

After several turns of the waltz, Morris bumped into the podium behind him.

Anna stumbled into him, catching her feet on the front of her bridesmaid dress. "Sorry, I always dance with my eyes closed," she said, not yet willing to confess her secret.

Standing in place, they were passed by the bride and groom, who, giddy with love and the belief that the war would soon end, were giggling uncontrollably.

"You'll learn to use the wall to feel your way in new places," Anna said. "At home, you'll count steps and memorize where things are. You'll read in Braille."

She could have said: *I had measles when I was ten, a rare infection of the optic nerve,* but she disliked explaining. His clumsiness reminded her of the days she couldn't walk across a room without bruising her shins on a chair leg. Swinging doors smashed into her face, a dropped toothbrush was lost forever, the fear of venturing outside alone, intense. In the beginning she cried frequently, despising her imperfect body, resenting her fate.

"Thank God you aren't saying you're sorry I was injured. I hear that a lot." He pulled her into his arms and held her close. She could sense him smelling her hair. In a moment his embrace would be noticed by others.

Her two teachers at Perkins School for the Blind, both unable to see since birth, were married to each other. They had a sighted son whom she had played with after school. When she was first blind and had asked her mother, would anyone have a blind woman for a wife, her mother said she would marry like anyone else.

She inhaled, touching her breasts to his chest, and wrapped her arms up around his neck. She felt his belt buckle press up against her. She breathed in deeply the scent of the freshly washed shirt, enhanced by the warmth of his body. His hot breath in her ear beat like a drum over the music. She forgot, for a moment, how afraid she was for the groom, for all his other friends, going back into battle.

She said, "I'm blind too," but her voice was lost in the loud clapping when the first dance ended.

"Need to take dance lessons Morris?" a voice behind them said. It was Gus, the malice in his voice unmistakable.

Anna took Morris's arm and tried to lead him away.

Gus taunted them with a mean parody of the tune from a nursery rhyme: "Two blind mice, two blind mice, see how they stumble, see how they fall."

Anna thought how sad: Gus's idea of a joke, teasing two blind people.

Morris said, "I danced, didn't I, Gus."

There was a pause.

Morris said to Anna: "Are you… Are *you* blind?"

Anna tried to explain. "Yes, but it shouldn't matter. I'm fine and you'll be fine too." She was full of regret for not telling him earlier.

He said nothing for a moment.

Then his arm was gone and the air before her filled with emptiness. Her sister, smelling of champagne, arrived at her side. The sounds of louder-than-usual chatter between songs and the offer of a chair from the groom let her know how Morris felt about her blindness.

For years afterwards, when she smelled Brylcreem on a man's hair, she would feel the familiar longing, remember the warmth of his arms and the touch of the light, magic fingers that made Morris so different. But at night, in her dreams, the memory of Morris frightened her. In his breathing, she had heard the echo of exploding bombs.

Interrupted Play

Uncle lived at Grandma's house which smelled of peanut butter cookies, Grandpa's cigar smoke and her old poodle who suffered from incontinence. Mother, overwhelmed by the care of my younger brother and twin baby sisters, sent me there often. I slept and played in the basement where, during the day it was dim as a saloon in a John Wayne western. The one window near the basement ceiling was mottled from the lawn sprinkler outside that Grandma said Grandpa never aimed properly. Grandma spent a good deal of her day yelling at Grandpa for his errors. She was a large woman with straight thin lips and eyes that rarely smiled. Mother said Grandma was never the same after she lost a baby to scarlet fever.

One night, after Grandma, Grandpa and the dog were asleep, Uncle slipped down the stairs to my basement bedroom to play. Grandma was strict about early bedtimes and we felt daring, breaking the rules.

Uncle and I had played together since we were innocents, his seven years my senior qualified him as a cool older brother. Uncle's four brothers and sisters, including my mother, were at least eighteen years older than he was. Mother once remarked to my father that Uncle was Grandma's "change of life baby." I had no idea what she meant, but I knew that Grandma and Grandpa were old to have a boy of sixteen. That June, Uncle went around the house singing "Rock Around the Clock," while beating the rhythm on chair backs and door jambs with the drum sticks he always carried.

The doll we played with that night had fully jointed arms and legs and a movable soft vinyl head. We called her *Baby*. I took off her blue cotton dress, panties and shoes and tucked her naked doll body inside my flannel nightgown, next to my belly, pretending the bulge was a live baby growing inside me. Uncle reached under the gown between my legs and slid her down my legs and out onto the sheets, helping her to be born. I had begun to develop two pointed nipples and I liked the sensations, squeezing the doll between my legs. I knew no words to describe what I was doing.

I did not think about what Uncle was doing beyond playing doctor. In those days, before iPhones and the internet, a boy of sixteen could remain naïve. Uncle was tall and blonde, with no whiskers on his cheeks; I am certain he had yet to be kissed by any girl who put her tongue in his mouth. He hated school and his grades were low, so to keep him out of trouble Grandma sent him off to band camp where he learned to properly play drums. Sixty-three years later, at his memorial service, over two hundred people showed up, to honor him as a band leader, teacher, and composer.

But all that happened much later, after Grandma found us.

The poodle had made a mess in the night and the smell of urine woke her up. Hearing our whispers, Grandma came downstairs, turned on the ceiling light and in its glare she stared at the two of us together on the bed. Uncle pulled his hand out from under my nightie, said goodnight and scrambled upstairs to his room. The doll fell on the floor. Grandma told me to go to sleep, turned off the light and left.

Very soon after she discovered us Uncle was spirited off to band camp and we never played with dolls again.

I didn't think about our interrupted play until years later when I had my own daughter. I believe Grandma saved both our lives. Sometimes it's just one moment when children turn in a wrong direction and can be lost forever.

Calming Properties of Ice Cream

On Sunday, May 24, 2020, I meet Gram's friend, Ralph.

COVID deaths in the United States near 100,000. Over 350,000 deaths are reported worldwide. The New York Times fills the entire Sunday front page with death notices of 1,000 U.S. victims.

Sunday morning, over coffee, I read an example from my laptop screen to Gram: "Alan Lund, 81, Washington, a conductor with the most amazing ear."

"Poor Alan Lund," she says. "My Ralph is 81."

I notice she calls him *My* Ralph.

After dinner every night Great Grandma Rose goes into the bedroom, behind a closed door, to talk on her phone with Ralph. When I ask about him, she says he is "just a friend" in a peculiar end-of-conversation way. (Confession: I keep a secret from Gram too. She's pretty conventional and I worry it will change how she sees me.)

I call her Gram, though she's my great-grandmother on Mom's side. Gram sits across from me in her old leather wing chair, which in our family we lovingly call her throne. I lugged that heavy chair up the front steps to my small, two-bedroom rental. She would not leave it at Shady Pines, her nickname for where she lives, a retirement home in Palo Alto. When the news reported COVID spreading in retirement communities, I kidnapped Gram and her chair, stuffed my duffel bag with her clothes, her medicines, and a handful of her favorite family photos, and brought her to my house to protect her. We have been sheltering in place for 69 days. So far, we have not killed each other.

"Sophie, we need ice cream," she says. Gram has maintained for years that ice cream is the key to longevity.

In my small living room Gram's White Linen perfume permeates the air with its pleasant lavender smell, not cloyingly floral like some. This familiar aroma, something I have known all my twenty-three years, relaxes me. She wears her green sweatshirt with the white ducks walking across the front and it brings out the green in her hazel-green eyes. She has a drooping eyelid from aging that makes her right eye smaller than the left; it doesn't interfere with her vision, but it gives her the friendly appearance of a slight wink when she smiles.

"We need ice cream," she says again. "Mint chip."

Gram repeats herself a lot, but I'm used to it. She has short term memory problems, will often forget what she's had for breakfast or things I've just told her, but she remembers the past with the details of a historian.

I drop a scoop of mint chip into her coffee mug. Mint chip is *so Gram:* the calming properties of peppermint with surprising bursts of chewy chocolate.

On June 15, 2020, Great Grandma Rose will be one hundred years old. Thankfully, Gram is in amazing shape—although she claims the number of artificial parts in her body exceeds her ability to count. She's had both knees and both hips replaced, but she does use a walker for balance, and she needs help putting on her shoes. The walker has already required repositioning of furniture in my small living room, but I was happy to drag my two chairs and a table out of the way rather than risk her falling. I've been grateful I have wood floors instead of carpeting. For her special day, we had arranged a celebration at Gamble Garden in Palo Alto. Family members had planned to travel from all over the United States for her party. Now, of course, travel is restricted, group gatherings prohibited, and the party has been cancelled.

I take a meditation breath and walk over to my front window. I never used to look out this window much, but lately I feel like a prisoner who craves the light. Overnight the dogwood tree, whose branches curl across the glass outside, developed yellow flowers. Blooming trees, spring in Palo Alto. Spring does not know there is a virus. Behind me I hear the soft sound of snoring, with that slight wheeze I recognize as normal. The ice cream is gone, and Gram has fallen asleep in her chair.

Last night, two different neighbors had their cars broken into and searched for cash. Before COVID I didn't know many neighbors. I'm a keep-to-myself kind of person. (Confession: I'm painfully shy around strangers.) Once Gram joined me, and I took her out to walk around the neighborhood with her walker, she encouraged stopping, waving, talking at a safe distance, and one by one we met the neighbors. Gram isn't shy about her age and most people haven't met anyone almost one hundred. These neighbors emailed us about the break-ins. One neighbor kept a twenty and some coins in the glove compartment and the money (though nothing else) was taken. It turned out these neighbors did not lock their cars (I always do), but the idea of someone going up and down the street "testing" for open cars at 3 a.m. looking for money was unsettling and sad. I hated to think any person was that desperate.

By the end of April, the U.S. economy lost 20.5 million jobs. They say it's the largest and most sudden decline since the government began tracking job data in 1940. I work as an IT assistant at the local gym and I've been furloughed indefinitely. Gram worked hard raising kids and keeping house. When my great-grandfather died, she took the life insurance money and laddered it in safe and reliable certificates of deposit. Without Gram's financial help, I could be out there too, checking unlocked cars for cash.

Sunday afternoon, I see a tall—very tall—Black man with a white beard, wearing a tank top, shorts and a Warriors cap standing outside on the sidewalk in front of my house, staring, some might say *loitering*. My thoughts go immediately to the car break-ins. (Confession: I am deeply ashamed of this reaction.) Gram has a look of combined pleasure and panic. Later she explains that she is "tickled pink" that Ralph has walked over from Shady Pines, and, at the same time, "alarmed" over the risk of neighbors calling the police.

In one of his former lives, Ralph was an African prince who left his country to get educated at Harvard. He moved to California, became a trial attorney, then a professor at the Santa Clara University School of Law, and, after he retired, a writer of murder mysteries. His pen name is Mazy Mitchell. I've read a few of her—I mean his—books on summer vacations. I am thrilled to meet Mazy Mitchell, who doesn't look at all like her dust jacket photo.

It's racist to admit that I expected Ralph to be a white man, but I don't remember Gram ever talking about any Black friends. I realize there are interesting things I don't know about Gram. (Confession: I begin to hope that Gram might accept my secret more than I thought.) Later she tells me she loved Ralph the first moment she heard his voice. She hates loud noises, has sensitive ears. Loud sounds cause a shock to her nervous system. She says Ralph has a soft, whispery voice that makes you lean in, pay attention, listen.

Waving out the window at him, Gram says, "Help! Quick! Get my walker. If we go outside, and talk to him, it will be clear to the neighbors he's here to visit us."

I hear the police siren as I'm walking out the front door carrying the walker. Gram struggles out behind me holding on to the handrail at the front steps. I don't know which neighbor called them, but I have my suspicions.

As the police car rolls up, Ralph puts his hands up expecting the worst. He's leaning forward, getting ready to fall onto his knees. I guess he's had this experience before.

All I know is that this is the man who has been keeping my Gram happy during the pandemic. Before the door on the police car opens, before Ralph can actually kneel, before I can think about the fact that I forgot to put on my mask, that I'm supposed to keep a safe physical distance of six feet—before any of that—I drop the walker and I race toward him.

I run up to Ralph and I hug him.

I'm pretty tall but I have to stand on my toes. He smells like fresh rainwater with a hint of popcorn. I knock off his cap in my enthusiasm. When he looks at me, he has wrinkles around his eyes that make them look like they are part of a permanent smile.

It is obvious to any idiot that I'm not hugging the thief they expect, and these police officers are nice people. When a man and a woman get out of the police car, Gram has already started her charm on them, waving from the front steps. By the time they leave we know all about them. Joe Brown has four kids. His wife is a nurse, *a pandemic hero* he calls her. Amara Mohan is single, my age, just started on the force, one of only two women. After meeting a few minutes (physical distance restored), thanks to Gram they know all about us too, including Ralph's history as a mystery writer.

Before Ralph leaves, he throws a farewell kiss toward Gram. She's so short her head must come only halfway up his chest. They are distancing (is that a verb now?) so I can't tell for sure.

Why didn't Gram tell me about Ralph sooner? Why was she so secretive?

"It's not that he's a Black man," she says, "it's that he's nineteen years younger. Robbing the cradle at one hundred." She laughs, making a joke of it. Then she says something beautiful: "Love at one hundred has transformed me, Sophie. Like a burst of major chords can change the nature of a song."

Love. I hope to know love like that. I'm thinking about Amara Mohan. She has a beauty mark on her throat that moves up and down when she speaks.

(Confession: I asked Amara for her phone number.)

That evening, Gram says we are allowed to have a medicinal glass of wine with our ice cream because Dr. Fauci from the NIH says alcohol is useful before and after White House COVID briefings.

Two scoops later, I open up to Gram that I like to have sex with women. She says she guessed that a long time ago. She's glad I'm ready to talk about it.

(Confession: I am so relieved I begin to cry.)

The Surprising Effect of a Dewy Grass Bath

Kristin stopped typing to breathe. She did her best to work, but when she thought about Asha's illness the shaking started—and the difficulty breathing. Her mind felt stretched and warped and letters on the screen blurred. She heard her heart pumping rapidly; the sound of its loud thumping against her breastbone caused a wave of fear. A voice in her mind repeated: *This cannot be happening. This cannot be happening.* To calm the panic, she turned her eyes out the window and took deep belly breaths.

Outside her single-pane glass window two bees were circling each other as if in a strange mating dance. Another bee bumped into the glass with its hairy feet close enough to touch; then a second, a third. She paused the recording she should have been transcribing, swept off her headphones and magnifying glasses, and leaned over to look. Holding her head close to the glass, squinting to compensate for her low vision, she watched the bees as they multiplied in numbers. She could see their squirming oval bodies with shocks of mustard-colored hair on their head and thorax, the striations of dark and light on the abdomen, black compound eyes, wings madly fluttering.

As she stared, a dozen more bees joined, flying in fast circles, generating a kinetic energy that reminded her of a turbine engine. She put her hand on the glass; it was warm. She could feel their buzzing vibrate the glass, tickling her fingers, as the glass shuddered when the bees struck its surface. As she stood frozen in awe, gazing at the brown squirming mass developing in front of her, the bees covered the window, blocking the sunlight. The room darkened.

Was this an omen? Good or bad?

Kristin called out to her wife: "Asha, you must come see this."

But Asha did not answer. Asha was lying down again. Another difficult day of chemotherapy. Spring was their favorite season, but not this year.

In their marriage Asha had always been the one taking care of Kristin. Born with albinism, Kristin had vision impairment. Asha did the driving, went to the grocery store, assumed all those chores that were difficult for Kristin to manage. Being older, more mature, she was Kristin's emotional rock, the grounded partner, her protector. Kristin's role was the fun spouse, the young one who entertained, who made Asha laugh. Kristin had developed strong audio skills and it was her standard joke that she "was not encumbered with sight" like Asha. But all that was *before*.

Frightened, unable to bear Asha's suffering, Kristin delayed going to check on her. She waited by the window as the bees began to disperse and the sunlight returned. Finally, a few bees, the last stragglers, remained on the glass, then lifted and circled each other before flying away.

The next day she discovered the swarm, a living, squirming nest of European honeybees, clumped together in a long oval ball the size of a huge watermelon, attached to their palm tree in the back yard. She ordered a wooden beehive online and once it arrived, she hired a team of professional beekeepers, Gerardo and Phoebe. They smoked the area to calm the bees. Next, they set a ladder next to the tree, climbed up, and cut down the swarm. Before introducing the bees to their hive, they brushed the bees gently into a cardboard box to find the queen. She was the largest bee, easily identified by her longer shape and pointed abdomen.

Phoebe carefully picked up the queen holding her by her wings. Using a Posca paint pen, she permanently marked her with a dab of white paint on her thorax; she explained all beekeepers do this to keep track of the queen so they know when a queen dies and a replacement occurs in the hive. All queens found in 2021 were marked with white.

"Think of it as her crown," said Phoebe, "she wears a white pearl."

Kristin and Asha named their honey bee queen Regina.

It was mid-summer, but instead of months, it seemed like years had passed since early spring when Kristin found the swarm. They sat under the shade of the terrace looking out on the garden; Asha had finished a phone call.

"Cancelled this week." She turned away, her face dark. Her platelets were low and the oncologist had delayed chemotherapy once again.

Kristin pressed a fallen sunflower head into Asha's hand, its petals drooping. The fuzzy disc florets where the bees loved to land tickled Kristin's fingers as she passed the flower to Asha. Asha smelled of bee smoke, a sweet scent of pine needles and spicy embers of sage she used to calm the bees while she tended to their new home.

Once the bees arrived, Asha became consumed with bee keeping, which Kristin accepted as a blessing. She thought, with a smile, that Asha looked like a bee with her yellow hair, short oval body, and tanned skin. Asha had dark and light striations on her belly too, birth marks from their daughter who died at birth, but Kristin did not like to talk about this wrenching subject. Kristin didn't want to bear children because she didn't want to pass on her albinism. After Asha was diagnosed, they stopped talking about having another child.

Kristin waited a moment, listening to the familiar buzzing near the sunflowers, feeling the hot sun on her forehead. She was overwhelmed with guilt, guilt at not being able to help manage the logistics of treatment, guilt at her angry, selfish thoughts when Asha was fighting cancer, guilt for being the healthy one.

She changed the subject, as she always did. "How is Regina today?"

"No signs of honey yet," said Asha, frowning. She hated that Kristin always pretended things were fine and never wanted to talk about difficult subjects. "The combs were stuck together again; I used the uncapping knife you bought."

Kristin knew it would take time for the bees to make honey in their new home; it annoyed her that Asha, in every conversation about her bees, kept repeating *no signs of honey yet*. "Their yellow poop is all over the walkway," said Kristin. "I don't appreciate the dirty mustard dots everywhere. I'll have to hose it again."

"You bought the damn beehive," said Asha. "Don't complain to me."

Kristin flounced off with her pruning shears to the sunflowers on the far side of the garden. Taller than the tallest sunflower, her white hair shone like a dome above them, curly, wild, in contrast to their perfectly formed circular yellows. She had on bioptic magnifying sunglasses with cat-eye tortoise frames. Behind the flamboyant frames she squinted her unusual sapphire eyes, which Asha had loved from the first moment they met. Covering her jeans and white tee, she wore her garden apron, red with multicolored tulips in abstract pots which, pulled in at her waist and flowing around her hips, gave her young body the round voluptuous look of an eighteenth-century oil painting—with her pale face, all she needed to look like an angel among the flowers was the wings. But—and she would be the first to confess—she was no angel.

She attacked the sunflower stems, slicing with her shears, cutting wildly, without precision. She tossed a dozen drooping heads together into her bucket knowing the crowded heads would quickly dehydrate. She stood in the bright sun without her hat, risking damage to her pale skin. Not caring, on purpose.

From across the garden, behind the fountain where two shiny emerald hummers splashed their wings, bathing, Asha coughed. The sound of her dry rasp mixed with the birds chirping and the bubbling of the fountain brought tears to Kristin's eyes. Asha was wrapping her arms around herself, in a tight hug, as if holding onto her chest would help the poor left lung breathe, the left lung where they found the malignant tumor.

"Lung cancer," said Kristin to herself, as she continued to thrash sunflowers as if they were to blame. "And Asha never smoked anything."

Asha said she expected to die first because she was nine years older than Kristin, but not this way. Not at forty-one. She had never smoked, not like Kristin who had tried just about everything up her nostrils. Kristin still snuck away in the evenings, pretending to need a last walk in the garden at sunset, when she actually went to have a cigar. She smoked in the side yard, a small rectangular-shaped area about the size of their guest bedroom. A tall redwood slat fence separated it from any neighbor's view. The ground was covered by a previous owner with ugly pink concrete and Kristin had left the cheap white plastic table and two chairs they found when they moved in; she claimed it as her space for "meditation" when she needed to be alone.

Of course, Asha knew Kristin was smoking there; she could smell it on her skin, in her mouth, in the kiss Kristin offered in bed. This was in the old days. The *before* days. Now they rarely kissed and loving was delayed until Asha felt better.

"He's at it again," Asha yelled across the garden to Kristin. She lifted her arm toward the house next door and held up her middle finger. Their neighbor, Gerald Mudgett, looked down from his second-floor window, his big binoculars aimed at Asha. Kristin stopped thrashing the tall green stems and gave him the finger too.

Kristin had a theory that Mudgett had observed them one of those first nights when Kristin, in a celebratory mode after moving out of their cramped condo downtown, invited Asha outside to see the full moon. This was before the fountain they installed, before the beehive, and before the sunflowers when the back yard was one big square of grass with the lone palm tree in the corner. She took off her clothes and began to roll in the cool wet grass, tumbling freely back and forth. "On Jónsmessa, Midsummer's Night in Iceland, my ancestors celebrated the summer solstice by rolling in dew-covered grass. They thought it would bring them health," she said, laughing. "Take a grass bath with me, Asha."

At first frowning, mumbling about grass burns and itching, Asha eventually took off her clothes and joined Kristin, abandoning her usual reserve. One thing led to another in a moment of coming together they would remark on later as shocking in its intensity, smiling all the next day while thinking about the aphrodisiac effects of newly mown grass and the surprising effect of a dewy grass bath.

Later when they noticed Mudgett observing them repeatedly from his upstairs window, they realized he might have been watching them that first evening. When it became clear he was a Peeping Tom, they knocked on his door to complain. Mudgett had gray hair cut short and a long oval face wrinkled into a permanent frown. A drooping lid on his right eye gave him a sinister look.

When they asked him to stop spying on them, he said he was "bird watching" with a lewd leer. He claimed that what he did in his own house was none of their business and slammed the door in their faces. It turned out he *was* actually a "birder," belonged to the neighborhood chapter, so they didn't think they could successfully report him to the police. Kristin started calling him "Creepy Peeper."

Throwing down her garden tool, Kristin carted her sunflower bucket over to Asha and banged it on the ground next to her. "When you get over feeling sorry for yourself, see if you can muster up energy to arrange these. I'm going inside to start an audio file I got yesterday," she said.

She hated the nasty person she had become.

Kristin went into her office, turned on her computer and clicked on the recorded audio. Lined up across the side of her desk, was an assortment of dome magnifiers, her reading glasses, and screen magnifier to aid her vision in reading her transcription.

This filmmaker did not send her the accompanying film footage; he used her transcript to edit his film. Most documentary filmmakers were on a tight deadline and sent their work piecemeal, but this time she had the whole project. She sat back in her swivel chair, head on the head rest, eyes closed, not thinking yet about marking speakers or adding time codes. Before transcribing a word, she listened all the way to the end, open to the images that came to her mind, to the undercurrents in the speech, like looking deep into a river for stones, or swimming fish, or for sediment blurring the color of water. Eventually she would summarize the interview questions, though the answers had to be typed verbatim, including every cough, sigh, and throat-clearing. She was known as one of the best professional transcribers of film documentaries in the business.

The interviewer began by introducing his subject "The Living Room," the name of the support group provided by GO2 Foundation for Lung Cancer. "The Living Room" was live streamed to patients and their families all over the world once a month. It was unusual for an interviewer to take time to describe the scene, but it was clear he was moved by his topic. He described the room as a meeting place, as welcoming as his grandparents' house on holidays, with sofas, chairs, coffee tables, colorful rugs. He claimed he could smell his Nana's hot chocolate and home-baked cookies when he walked into the room. On a gray wall above a couch, where patients and others sat to talk, hung four huge capital letters, each with a white background overprinted with articles about patient support and success. The white letters, which stood out against the gray wall, formed the word "HOPE." He went on to introduce Bonnie J. Addario, a co-founder of the Foundation.

Kristin paused the recording. She had forgotten that this filmmaker had sent her this subject, suggesting it might have a personal interest for her and Asha. Asha had tried a support group in the beginning and came home depressed and angry. She claimed she would never go back.

When Bonnie Addario began to speak, Kristin was captivated by the sound. Her voice, the rich tenor of a woman in the prime of life, exuded vitality; she formed her sentences without fillers, without hesitancy. She was not afraid to pause and think before answering. Her survival story was courageous, riveting, inspiring, and by the time Kristin had finished the last words of the interview she found herself crying. Bonnie Addario said, "And for those who find themselves on this trail, know that I will be walking by your side, hand in hand, toward a brighter future dominated by a single word: Life."

Life, hope, cure—words Kristin had not allowed herself to say, pretending the cancer wasn't there would be the best way to make it disappear.

Kristin took off her clouded glasses and rubbed her eyes. It was the first time she admitted to herself that they needed help. *She* needed help. She searched online for GO2 Foundation and registered for the next month's virtual session.

The first thing Asha wanted to do when she got home from infusion treatment was sit outside in her garden, watching her bees. She was still sitting there at 5:30 in the evening when the Living Room session was scheduled to start.

"It's only an hour," said Kristin who took Asha's arm and pulled her up. She leaned down and kissed her hair. After infusions Asha always smelled vaguely like disinfectant. She brought home the white glare of clinic hallways, nurse uniforms, masks, the chill of the treatment room's low temperature, the lingering taste of this other world, outside nature, a chemical world.

Kristin gently put her arm around Asha's waist and walked her into the house, up the stairs, to her office. After she settled Asha in her most comfortable office chair, she put on the spectacle-mounted binoculars she used to watch videos and sat next to her in her desk chair. She clicked on YouTube Live to join the session.

The screen opened with printed text: "The Living Room—Bring Hope Home."

Bonnie Addario introduced herself. She was an attractive, energetic woman with round glasses sporting black and white striped cat-eye frames and she wore her auburn hair swept up into a modern shag style.

"Look, she has cat-eye frames like your sunglasses," said Asha. Asha liked her immediately.

Addario explained how survival rates from lung cancer had been increasing since she started her work with the Foundation, since more research had been funded, since the stigma of lung cancer's association with smoking had been slowly easing as more people realized that anyone could get lung cancer. Bonnie briefly told her story as a lung cancer survivor and then described her disappointing experience with her first support group which made her feel hopeless. She explained "The Living Room" was started to offer something different; to bring in oncologists and scientists to talk about research and treatment options, and patients and caregivers to share their stories. "The Living Room" would provide a place where people could gather to believe that surviving this disease was a possibility—a place to "bring hope home."

"When is your happiest time?" asked a woman, who appeared next. She had gray hair that fell past her shoulders and she wore a red sweater. She began with a wide, smile, showing bright white teeth. "What brings you joy?"

She introduced herself as Jaya, the younger sister of Swaytha, a survivor. "Though Swaytha had the cancer in her body and bravely faced treatment after treatment, being her caregiver was much harder than I imagined. I fell into depression. Then I met another caregiver through the GO2 Foundation; she gave me her secret. She said focus on finding joy, one moment of joy every day. Every day I found a thing of beauty to share: an aria we loved, Puccini's "Nessun Dorma" from *Turandot*, Bonnard's painting "Stairs with Mimosa," a Billy Collins poem, "The Genius," fresh-baked bread, salted caramel ice cream. It gave me purpose each day, something positive, something that wasn't giving the cancer any more space than it deserved. Remember, all of us, together in this journey, we are *not* the disease. We are *managing* the disease."

The session went on with reports about new discoveries in biomarking, but Kristin stopped listening. She leaned back against the head rest of her desk chair, closed her eyes. When was their happiest time? She knew immediately. She could smell the newly mown grass, could see the green all around her, could feel the cool, tickling blades next to her lips, the emotional sense of well-being, of fun, of play. It was the grass bath. The grass bath with Asha.

In the evening, after Asha was asleep, Kristin went into her office and sat again at the desk in front of her computer. She wanted to sit outside with a cigar, but she had promised herself to give up smoking. Instead, she stared out the window. She could hear the soothing water of her garden fountain bubbling like a small brook. She imagined Asha's bees waggle-dancing in their beehive, Regina the queen, wearing her white jewel, laying eggs, the creamy yellow honey dripping from the combs, harvested, spread over her morning toast, or licked from a dipped spoon. She imagined Asha healthy, her soft warm mouth open, lips full, the taste of honey in her kiss. Asha, a *survivor*.

Kristin thought about her smoking space, its privacy, with its convenient side door to the downstairs and gated fence. She went to the web and searched for "concrete removal." She took out a piece of paper and wrote down figures, estimated the square footage of her side yard. After removal, there would be the cost of an irrigation system, turf and drainage. It was an area that got full sun several hours a day; the turf would have to be a warm-weather grass. She searched for "the softest grass." Then she sketched the side yard. Around the perimeter, she drew steppingstones made of natural slate and a place for a wooden bench, where they could put their discarded clothing. In the center would be Emerald Zoysia grass, velvety soft for bare feet, refreshingly smooth for naked skin, perfect for dewy grass baths.

Finished with her planning, she looked out the window toward the palm tree, fronds lit by the moon, waving in the breeze. She remembered how the bees first swarmed outside this window. European honey bees weren't aggressive, but if they stung their venom could cause death in rare cases. She didn't wish Mudgett's death; she wished an allergic reaction—hives, itching, some dizziness, a welt or two. She imagined a team of her protective female bees swarming around Creeper Peeper's open upstairs window, stinging his binocular-holding arms, convincing him to sell his house and move.

She went to bed late that night. Closing her eyes, she felt her heart thumping, but at a normal pace. Asha was already asleep. She heard her whispered breathing, a comforting sound in the night. Kristin reached under the covers and took her hand. It was warm, soft, familiar. As Kristin interlocked their fingers, Asha squeezed back.

Part IV: Ultimate Mystery

Ghosts in the Grand Wardrobe

The immense Grand Wardrobe Box is big enough to hide a dead body.

Its dusty, cob-webbed exterior, its crushed bottom corner, its brand "U-Haul" fading into the brown cardboard, remind me of the pale, shriveled skin of a dead person. Standing next to this huge packing box, rising up as tall as my shoulder and three times wider than my slim self, in my head I hear a suspenseful crime scene soundtrack. I imagine a dead human thing, curled sideways, head bent, bloodied hair, arms and legs folded, tumbling out from the opened box, the kind of surprise one expects on watching the lid of a car trunk open in a streaming police procedural. I do not admit to my young roommate, who is helping me sort out the garage, that I, a mature woman well into her third age, am afraid of opening a twenty-year old packing box.

Using his always-handy Swiss Army Knife to cut the tape fastening the box closed, he says, "I wonder if a rat crawled in that hole at the crushed corner to nest. Remember, I had rats crawl up inside my Prius and eat the wiring."

"Lovely thought. So glad you shared that, Robbie."

As he unfolds and releases the top flaps, I prepare my nose for the odor of a dead rodent.

The opening reveals—not a rat—but the 24-inch metal hanging bar, sold as the prime benefit of this packing box. Crowded there, each covered in re-purposed plastic bags from a dry cleaner long out of business, are old clothes I saved when preparing my house for a remodel twenty-plus years ago.

Robbie waves me aside. "I'll do the heavy lifting. You do the deciding. Keep or donate. Those are your only choices."

I seek my folding chair in the corner and settle back against the cushion comforting my arthritic spine, grateful for his energy.

While he struggles to release the first piece of clothing from the overstuffed interior, I indulge in woolgathering, searching my brain for the memory of what I put in this box when I was that past woman, married to my favorite husband, in the thick of middle life and its abstractions, making space in my brain for paint colors and kitchen tile decisions. I accept some level of cognitive decline as inevitable, but it appears I have completely lost track of the contents of this box. Not remembering has its benefits: I imagine I am on an adventure with C. S. Lewis, my own "Lion, Witch and Wardrobe" story. I am Lucy, the ordinary child who enters a wardrobe and finds the magical world of Narnia. As a girl, I peeked in every closet with hope in my heart.

Robbie, always organized to perfection, has set up paper bags next to my chair in the hope that I will use them to donate everything we find to the thrift shop. He dreams, he has said, that the big box and its contents will no longer hog space in our shared garage. To replace his Prius, he has ordered a red Tesla Model Y, to arrive next month, and has plans to install a wall charger where the box stands now. I find his contribution to stopping climate change with an all-electric car admirable.

He doesn't know it but I plan to drive that car.

He lifts a garment out of the box, shakes off its plastic covering, walks over to my chair and holds it up for my decision. "Keep or donate," he orders. He's smiling, with that quirky, lopsided look I love.

I look up from my low chair, searching for his eyes, not noticing the clothing. "Did you know the word 'wardrobe' comes from the French 'warder' to keep or guard and 'robe' garment?" I admit I have mischief in mind. How lovely it would be to drop this chore immediately and go out for a coffee.

He knows that look. "Stay focused. Keep or donate?"

He presents a gray suit with padded shoulders, a very short skirt and executive collar rimmed in white, worn in a time when my business cards read "Senior Vice President." In those days I flew first class to make important presentations to various all-male Boards of Directors. Sitting in my garage in my yoga pants from Athletica, a comfortable tee shirt bra, and my New Balance Fresh Foam shoes, I am no longer that suited woman, but she served me well during my work life.

The wrinkled garment smells sour, like an alley way downtown. The metal hanger, padded with orange foam, loosens its desiccated pieces all over the suit and the garage floor. The released plastic bag blows around the garage like a trapped bird looking to escape the room.

"Donate," I say, shaking my head in disbelief at the size of the shoulder pads. It looks like something the actors wore on Inspector Morse episodes now streaming on Britbox. I confess I occasionally watch this classic, obtaining some relief from today's hard news, by a visit with John Thaw and hearing the beautiful Barrington Pheloung music, its morse code motif spelling out the name "M.o.r.s.e." a secret not everyone knows.

Robbie stuffs the suit in a bag for me, sweeps aside the trash accumulating on the floor, goes to the box again and this time he holds up a summer dress, sleeveless, its flower print a potpourri of young-girl colors, pink, blue, pale violet. Saved from my daughter's middle school graduation. I picture the family celebration afterwards, a meal at the Officers' Club at the Presidio in San Francisco (closed now), a buffet brunch, plates loaded with waffles drowned in maple syrup. Next, packed together, her white cap and gown with tassels in white and green, the Viking colors, from high school graduation.

I take out my phone and snap a picture. "I'll store the photo, not the clothes," I say. I do keep the tassels. I will send them to her later, my adult daughter, who lives a thousand miles away, in the thick of her middle life and its abstractions, as I once was.

Next. A hand-made (no label) black beaded dress, with a mid-calf length skirt, popular in the 1920s, often worn with a fascinator. Does this elaborate evening dress come from the chest that my mother kept with accessories from her past for my children to play dress-up? Memory fails me.

"Donate."

Next. A Camp Fire Girls uniform, brown cotton with leather fringe on the collar and hem, vintage, from the 1970s. I do remember earning those patches and wooden beads and metal badges. They were awarded for different tasks completed: orange for home craft, red for health, brown for camp craft, green for hand craft, blue for nature, yellow for business and red, white, and blue for citizenship.

"Donate?" he says.

I hesitate as I finger the beaded headband. Later I will find a Camp Fire Girls uniform offered on Etsy for $255. Mine is not in good shape, torn from when Grandma wore it for Halloween with a painted face and head feather, pretending she was a Native American, unintentionally so realistic she scared my then preschool age children into tears.

"Donate." I think some thrift-shop explorer will delight in finding this classic.

The Grand Wardrobe Box is advertised to hold two feet of closet garments. It is crammed with double that amount: winter coats with huge shoulders, a fake fur, party dresses with sparkles, another cap and gown (black, from my son's graduation), a tee shirt with my son's baseball photo, a Nehru shirt hand-sewn by my mother-in-law, gorgeous blue fabric around the collar, and many more. Robbie and I smell like unwashed clothes; our hands are black and we begin to sneeze. The garage floor is littered with plastic bags, metal hangers, crumbs of foam and bits of paper. Robbie is anxious to get on with cleanup and recycling. My back aches and calls for this to end. While we are working here, the afternoon has passed; it is dark, time to prepare dinner.

One more item remains.

"Well, well, well," he says. "I suppose you must keep this," To show me, he holds it up with both hands, draping it between both arms because of the long train. Its fabric, yellow with a tinge of cream, shines like silk in the pale overhead light.

I chose yellow rather than white, because it was my second marriage and those were the rules. Virginal white was appropriate only for the first time. My younger self was very conscious of following rules.

As I reach out to touch the train, I smile. Along the side of the fabric is a faint brown stain. "Spilled German chocolate cake," I say to Robbie. 'It was an unusual choice for a wedding cake, but your favorite. Remember?"

At this point I must make a confession: Robbie is actually my favorite husband and my best friend for fifty years. I like to *pretend* Robbie is my young roommate; it's my way of mentally spicing up my love life, like some couples wear costumes in the bedroom. No one has to know, not even Robbie. So, keep it our secret please.

Later, I will hang this dress outside to air it out and then pack it carefully away in a cupboard with cedar balls to protect it. I have let go of all the other garments, ready to donate them to the thrift shop for second-hand shoppers to discover, and the Wardrobe Box is now empty, ready for recycling. When my roommate has finished cleanup, and we've packed all the bags in the car, ready for the trip to the thrift shop tomorrow, we stand together at the door into the house, pausing to turn out the light.

Finger on the light switch, I hesitate, looking back at the empty box.

Like the Ghost of Christmas Past who visited Ebenezer Scrooge, each of these garments represented a different time in my life. Seeing them emerge from the Grand Wardrobe Box was like watching a movie with ghosts of my younger selves. I felt a mixture of grief and joy, inexplicable, yet liberating. Liberating to let it go. It's only stuff I tell myself; I keep the memories.

Robbie senses my mixed emotions and puts his arm around me.

He says, with his quirky smile, "I know your little secret. You plan to drive my Tesla."

Fallen Star

On a normal day our teacher in Room 212 of Denver's South High School was an educator who loved grammar more than he loved football. Pacing back and forth in front of his chalkboard covered with diagramed sentences, he would explain the dangers in dangling verbal phrases (*The Macmillan Handbook of English*, third edition, page 469, 44a.). He grasped the spine of his open grammar book in one hand and, gesticulating with the other, revealed its secrets, as excited as if this were a murder mystery and we were about to discover the identity of the killer. He meticulously corrected every piece of student writing with codes to direct us to the appropriate usage in the grammar book. His enthusiasm for sentences polished like silver remains with me today. On Saturday afternoons in the fall, he could be spotted in the bleachers of the football field marking student papers in red while he cheered for the team. At sporting events, like every day in class, he wore a suit, white shirt, and tie.

But on this April day, hands shaking, tears in his eyes, a middle aged, balding man with his striped tie hanging loose stood in front of the chalkboard clutching a student's paper, a story written for the class assignment we had been given before spring break. I sat at the front desk in the row nearest the wall. Though I did not know why, I sensed this was an important reading. I pulled my skirt down attempting to cover knobby knees, a habit when nervous. In photos from my 1963 yearbook, I look younger than seventeen, eyes hidden by thick glasses I detested, lips drawn straight in a serious line over my father's square chin. I was an innocent teenager. Until that moment I believed death could not touch me.

Our teacher leaned against the chalkboard, one shoe on the floor, the other shoe on the wall below, as if he needed extra support. As he read the words on the page, he stuck one hand in his suit coat pocket where he collected a hoard of broken chalk pieces; he handled them as he spoke. We watched as his hand clenched and unclenched against the inside of the fabric. The story was about a teenage boy who got lost in the Rocky Mountains in a snowstorm while hiking and died of exposure. Lying on the frozen ground, looking up at the night sky, the boy's last sight was a falling star.

The student's desk was behind mine. In September, on the first day of class, I noticed him immediately. He was pleasantly tall, had slightly protruding ears, puppy eyes and thin lips. A boy who belonged out of doors, confined in the classroom, overflowed with repressed energy. Long legs folded under his desk, he constantly kicked the air with his right foot, frequently landing on the chair legs of my desk. I hear his whisper: *Sorry. Oh, sorry.* A polite, gentle boy, he apologized at least ten times during any class period.

In October the boy invited me to the homecoming dance. His kiss goodnight at my door was what my girlfriends called a *grab and smash*. He liked me and he was nervous. If we had been in the mountains, he would have been more at home. His passion for the night sky might have inspired him.

This April day his desk was empty.

We all knew, from the newspapers on Sunday, our classmate fell and broke his neck while hiking with a friend near Estes Park.

His loss was more than the loss of a friend, the loss of shared memories, the loss of a life of promise, though it was all those things. Like a falling star, a foreboding, at seventeen, his passing was my first evidence of cosmic unrest.

When our teacher finished the boy's story, there was complete silence in the room. No one could believe the strange coincidence that the boy wrote the mountain story so near his own death in those same mountains. No one could believe he was gone. I tried to imagine the long legs that had kicked my desk lying on the ground, flung askew, forever stilled.

Our teacher turned his bent head to the wall and fumbled with his glasses. On his lower back, the nap of his brown suit coat was imprinted with the white chalk from a diagrammed sentence.

Birds on the Water

The birds on the water have not heard him yet. Once they do, they will burst upwards in flight and he will pull the trigger. A gaggle of nine geese, necks huddled, drifts near the opposite bank. For a second the old farmer smells stuffed goose, roasted on a spit. He kneads feathers on his fingers from cleaning past kills. The illusions—a warm fire, the taste of mulled wine, the shelter of his chair after a good meal—are seductive. But he will not aim at the birds today.

At home he has the spit ready behind the kitchen, the fire laid. His wife, Ingrid, assembled all the materials for a fruit and chestnut stuffing—twelve ounces of pitted prunes, an orange, three apples and a dozen chestnuts. She left these ingredients out on the kitchen counter as they agreed—for proof it was an accident when the police question him.

Goran Pettersson points the rifle away from the geese and looks again into the scope. Across the lake, still as glass, a doe stretches her neck toward the sky. The old farmer sees her ears pivoting, detecting. But he will not aim at the deer today.

The birds on the water have not heard him yet. The rifle is hard against his shoulder, the smell of gun oil burns his throat, and a rain of tears drowns his jaw. Goran does not want to enter his next minute. So, he holds his breath.

Ingrid stands several yards ahead of him on the brown grassy slope of the hill where the birds will fly when they launch. She leans against her walking stick. She is as motionless as the doe but is looking away toward the horizon where the sun begins to light. Goran turns the rifle toward her. In the scope he sees the long braid of her gray hair magnified, like a woven afghan—shades of silver, gray, ash blonde, white. He feels its familiar windings slide across his hand, from the thousand times he's pulled her toward him.

She is ten years older and from the beginning he always did what she said. Some called her bossy, but he never minded her ways. He knew he was prone to temper, easy to rile if things weren't as expected, impatient around children. It was her decision not to have any. When they were younger and her father eventually died from the plaques and tangles in his brain, they began talking of their own deaths—in theory. One afternoon on a picnic, after wild loving on that same grassy hill—in the hour afterwards when he was always so grateful and would say yes to anything she asked—he had agreed to save her the agony of a long dying.

Now she stands there, watching the sun rise, trusting him completely.

The weight of the promise he made cuts into his spine. When the rifle fires he fears his body will split, like a tree fractured in its fall.

Finally, he has to breathe. His exhale rustles the long grass where he stands.

The birds on the water burst upwards in flight.

But he lowers the rifle.

When he does not fire, Ingrid turns, braces against her walking stick, and looks at Goran. After a while she shuffles down the hill toward him. He is afraid of her stare as she advances, that he has failed her, failed in his promise. He feels sweat run down his side, making his chambray shirt damp under his coat. His knees turn pliant and his lungs ache with the shame that has settled on him.

But she walks past. Her eyes gaze blank, two holes in her face. She has forgotten why they came.

He does not know what to do so he goes about his day. He mends the fence by the garden, sweeps the chicken pen, and picks ripe tomatoes for dinner salad. Sometimes, since he sold his cropland, keeping only his house and the property by the lake, he has to search for things to occupy his time. He does his chores slowly so they will last longer.

From outside he observes Ingrid through the windows. She passes back and forth behind the glass inside each room. He knows she will dust first and then vacuum. Sometimes, forgetting, she will dust again, starting over.

They roast a chicken for dinner. He makes the stuffing. Afterwards they sit with coffee mugs at the wooden kitchen table in their two straight-back chairs while the sun descends, darkening the room about them. Her hand lies still on the tabletop. He cups his hand over hers.

Many mornings pass. Every morning Ingrid asks to walk to the lake.

This new morning the birds on the water do not hear him yet. The birds on the water might be the same geese, older, or they might be descended from last year's goslings or they might be new birds, just landed. The deer's ears pivot in the scope, or it might be a jack rabbit with a twitching nose, or it might be a bob cat, still as a stone, anticipating prey. The rifle is the same rifle and it is loaded. Goran puts his finger gently on the trigger.

His wife stands several yards ahead of him on the brown grassy slope of the hill. She is the same wife, but she is not the same wife.

The birds on the water have not heard him yet. He does not want to enter his next minute, or the next, or the next. So, Goran holds his breath.

Miles to Go

Once I read a book. It was Christmas Eve and Billie could not sleep. I found him sobbing in the hallway outside the room where I slept when a guest at my son's house. Billie's long curly brown hair, which he did not allow anyone to trim, stood tousled on his head, a sign of multiple turns on his hot pillow. He wore the red and green dinosaur-patterned jammies I gave him which proved to be a size too big, the arms dripping down over his hands. He looked up at me with his big brown, long-lashed, baby-sad eyes. For a moment it was the face of his father, and I was transported in time to forty years past. But like a flash that boy was gone, and there was Billie, who at six was absolutely his own man.

"What if I can't sleep all night, Gran?" he said. He'd been told Santa would not come until everyone went to sleep.

Before Billie went to bed, my son's house was so full of anticipation it seemed to lean off the Marin hillside toward the moon, over which, later that night, Santa would fly, guiding his sleigh toward a soft landing on the roof. The air smelled of sticky buns rising in the oven and peppermint candy canes hanging from the fireplace mantlepiece, warmed by the gas fire. Billie's black and white cat, Checkers, chased a ball ornament he had pawed off the lower branches of the decorated Christmas tree and Billie's frantic parents, doing last-minute gift wrapping, ran out of scotch tape and had to borrow from the neighbors—none of this was a calming preparation for sleep.

A widow for five years, insomnia regularly interrupted my nights so I was sympathetic. But I retired from nursing long ago, lived alone since my Robert died and no one depended on me. What if Santa couldn't come until I slept? The pressure to sleep would be enormous—exactly when sleep was impossible. Poor Billie.

I could see the words "I want my Mam…" begin to form on his pursed lips as Billie's chest heaved with a spasm. He turned toward his parents' bedroom. His Mama and Papa were busy behind their closed door, stuffing candy in stockings, assembling a scooter, adding batteries to a remote-control car.

If he opened his parents' door, at risk was the magic of believing, something he would question soon enough. I put my arms around his tiny frame, pulled him gently into my bedroom, and closed the door. "Let's read a book together," I said.

I pulled back the covers and Billie slid into my bed. He snuggled down into the quilt, his red nose visible, his eyes still wide with tears. I slipped in next to him, marveling how his small body was as cozy as a blanket straight from the warming cabinet.

I picked up a large picture book left on the table next to my bed, the Robert Frost poem, *Stopping by Woods on a Snowy Evening*, illustrated by Susan Jeffers. I had read Frost's famous poem often during my seventy-odd years, but this was the first time in a book illustrated for children. As I opened the book, I paused a moment to appreciate the feel of the slippery pages on my fingers and the vague scent of vanilla and almond lingering on the night air, grateful to the ghost of the coniferous tree who gave its life to the pulp-making.

Checkers jumped up onto the bed. The cat had managed to slip in before we closed the door; he knew he was not allowed in this room as he liked to eat the prohibited fern on the nightstand.

"Let him stay, Gran," pleaded Billie.

Checkers turned around three times, then curled up on top of my feet. He put his head on his paws. The music of his purring filled my ears, rumbling like a drum buzz roll.

Whose woods these are I think I know. His house is in the village though.

The words of Frost's timeless poem dripped off my lips like warm chocolate. Billie's crying stopped. In the soft light of the bedside lamp, the drying tears made shiny trails down his cheeks. I squeezed his small hand under the covers.

He will not see me stopping here. To watch his woods fill up with snow.

I whispered these words into the eyes of a huge snowy owl who stared back at me from a tree limb. With these words and the illustrations before us, a snowy winter forest populated our imaginations with the owl, rabbits, several deer, a fox, and an old man. The man Susan Jeffers put in her illustrations had a white beard and a colorful cap and scarf and Billie asked, "Is that Santa?"

I said, "What do you think?"

Billie wasn't sure. His forehead crinkled as he pondered this question. A horse pulled this man's sleigh instead of reindeer.

"Look at the snow," he said, appearing worried. "It's snowing all over the page. Won't the owl freeze?"

"Snowy owls have feathers everywhere to keep them warm," I explain. "Even their feet are covered with feathers; their feet look like your fluffy slippers."

On the next page the rotund old man who might be Santa was lying down, sweeping his arms in semi-circles, making a pattern in the snow. His moving about surprised the owl who flew across the page. Below the owl two rabbits, a squirrel, and two chipmunks looked cold and hungry.

"But what will the animals eat?" Billie sat up, anxious.

"He's making a snow angel," I said to distract Billie. "Look." I pointed to the shape of the wings.

"But Gran, how will they survive?" Billie tugged at my sleeve. I kept reading.

My little horse must think it queer. To stop without a farmhouse near. Between the woods and frozen lake. The darkest evening of the year. He gives his harness bells a shake. To ask if there is some mistake.

"Why do you think he stopped?" Billie tugged at my sleeve again. "Even his horse wonders what he is doing."

99

The next page had a drawing of the old man; his head had disappeared under the blanket that covered the back of the sleigh. He searched for something he put there.

"What is he doing?" said Billie. "What does he have in the sleigh?"

His desire to know was urgent.

Billie and I leaned forward to look closely at the picture, to see what the old man who might be Santa was doing. The old man reached under the blanket on his sleigh and took out a bag of seeds, grass, and branches. He walked over to the tree where the owl had perched and spread them on the ground. He fed the animals and, in that cold, snowy winter forest, they would not go hungry.

Billie's hand felt limp and relaxed and his body lightened. I understood that in his mind everything clicked into place. Checker's purring blended with his Gran's soft voice like a lullaby. Everything that mattered was there in his house and he was safe. As he closed his eyes, I read: *The only other sound's the sweep of easy wind and…* On his cheek, my finger traced the kiss of *downy flake.*

As Billie slipped, slowly, softly, gently into dreams, Frost's last words echoed in the room like an evening prayer.

The woods are lovely, dark and deep
But I have promises to keep
And miles to go before I—

I didn't often think of my age, and rarely felt old, but at my next birthday I would be seventy-seven. As I pulled the covers up over Billie's shoulders, I whispered: *But I have promises to keep, and miles to go before I sleep.*

Yes. Please. *Miles to go.*

Ultimate Mystery

One timeless afternoon she sits at her dying mother's bedside, lost in the gentle white noise of the oxygen concentrator which she will wrongly remember for the rest of her life as the sound of the sea. The hospice nurse interrupts to give her a pamphlet which describes the signs of impending death. Her mother is at peace, and does not appear to feel pain, but the nurse says her time is short. Joanne, or Jojo as her mother calls her, knows about dying from the death of her father, and the death of her husband. She skims over the familiar list of signs: *Not eating or drinking, changes in breathing, fever, withdrawal.*

The woman in the bed next to Jojo's chair resembles her mother less and less. Her hair, once chestnut brown, spreads on the pillow, grayed and thinned. The grooves in her pale cheeks deepen when she smiles, eyes closed, lids fluttering with her morphine dreams. With eyes of love, Jojo sees all the mothers she has known in her lifetime, from young mother to wise great grandmother, lying there in transparent layers in the white sunlight that feathers the air.

Scanning the pamphlet, she stops at one section: *Coolness: Hands, arms, feet, and legs, increasingly cold to the touch… the color of the skin may change… become mottled.*

In *War and Peace*, Tolstoy described Prince Andrei's death as "the last spiritual struggle between life and death, in which death gained the victory." She wishes she had that book in front of her instead of these stark words, written by a social worker, that give no mention of the spirit.

Jojo's hands feel like ice, *fingers numb*, though it is pleasantly warm in the room from a space heater the nurse requested to supplement the old furnace in her mother's ancient house. She feels *breathless*, as if she's been running. She tosses the pamphlet onto her mother's medicine table, needing nothing more from it.

The afternoon creeps by, disappearing into time passed.

She hears her mother's heartbeat, but no, it's the big clock in the hall. She smells flowers, but no, it's the aide in the kitchen making jasmine tea. She feels *feverish*, but no, she's cold. She pulls her sweater close. Scattered, her mind flails around, searching for what to say in the obituary. Her hand moves back and forth across her lap, as if she is holding a pen and writing: Florence Joanne Ferguson labored thirty-five years as a telephone operator for New Jersey Bell. At home, she grew azaleas, rhododendron, and holly, and sold them in her husband's nursery. Flo attended church, made apple pies that won awards, raised one daughter. Every year, until he died, she escaped the East Coast winters by travelling with her husband to an Airstream park in Florida. Do these details of home baking and RV travels reveal anything about the complex woman who was her mother? Do they capture her temper when unexpected events changed plans, her obsession with being on time, the way she turned away from expressing her emotions?

The nurse offers her tea, but she refuses, *unable to imagine eating or drinking*.

In her lifetime her mother witnessed the Great Depression, a world war, and the invention of the computer. In the year of her birth women achieved the right to vote. Two months ago, she waved out her window at a drive-by birthday celebration of her 100th birthday, attended by friends from her church. The line of cars was longer than the line of cars waiting for COVID tests, she said proudly that night, as they watched the pandemic news on television.

Because her knees ache, Jojo stands to stretch. At seventy-five, her joints beg for replacement, but she delays care of herself. Short, like her mother, she shares with her the social challenges of being small: feeling claustrophobic in a crowd, being unable to reach high shelves in stores, envying the debonaire tallness of fashion models. They both could tell stories of exasperation as men patted them on the head, as if they were children. Yet being small and attractive had its benefits too; people guessed their age as much younger. They shared rich thick hair, a turn of the nose, sparkling brown eyes.

Strangers thought they were sisters. "But this doesn't belong in an obituary," Jojo whispers to herself, smiling.

As a child, without brothers and sisters, Jojo was treated like another adult in the house. The plants and flowers her mother loved became the drawings that her daughter made when she was three, evolving into a career as an artist, and in later years, as an art teacher. She reseeded her mother's flowers, not in the earth, but on parchment in watercolor paints. Once an adult, Jojo and her mother switched roles back and forth: Jojo was mother to Flo, Flo was mother to Jojo, depending on who had the expertise or the need. When her father died, Jojo promised him she would take care of her mother. Slowly, as time passed, and her mother aged, Jojo was more often doing the mothering. She never regretted a moment of this. When her children grew up and moved on, and her husband died, she was not alone. Her mother needed her, and she had promised.

Jojo looks at her mother's hands. *They are turning a mottled purple.*

She kneels next to the bed and takes her mother's cold hand in hers. She looks down at her fingers interlocked with her mother's fingers. *They are turning a mottled purple.*

The room around her falls away. She and her mother are on the shores of a Sistine sea, luminous under a hanging moon. Wind whispers in her ears, like the hum of a choir. She hears the surf rising, the crash of waves against sand, feels the dark water coming closer and closer. The advancing tide closes over their heads, but they are held safe in the barrel of a breaking wave. In the last seconds, as her mother's death approaches, their hands wind together in the white halo of moonlight, repeating the miracle they shared at birth, closing the circle of life, experiencing together the ultimate mystery.

"And the end of all our exploring will be to arrive where we started and know the place for the first time."

~ T.S. Eliot, *Four Quartets*

Acknowledgements

My heartfelt gratitude goes to my brother and sister, my children, and my friends for their love and encouragement. I thank Alice LaPlante and my dedicated teachers at Stanford Continuing Studies, the editors of literary journals who published my stories, my friend and amazing writer, Aggie Zivaljevic, and my independent bookstore, Kepler's Books. I thank Robin Stratton at Big Table Publishing for her generous editorial guidance. Special thanks to the A-Z Writing Group, Tristen Chang's Story Class, and my Dream Group for taking the journey with me. I thank Alison Davis, Bonnie Addario, Christie Cochrell, Evy Schiffman, Jackie Krantz, Sharlene Carlson, Sheila Settle, Tony Press, Westley Althouse and his cats (Chuck and Walker) for their story inspirations and generous permissions. And, finally, to the one who finds himself in every story, thank you, favorite husband, Mike.

I am grateful to the following literary journals who first published these stories, listed in the order of appearance in the collection.

"Love Child," in *Amarillo Bay*

"Stand Up," in *Menda City Review*

"#theprocedure," in *Permafrost Magazine*

"Big Lies," in *Gravel*

"Cool Shirt," in *Flash, The International Short-Short Story Magazine*

"Caught in Headlights," *Grand Dame Literary*

"Sin of Omission" was first published as "Today, Five Years Hence," in *Write Yourself Out of a Corner*, by Alice LaPlante

"A Conversation Between Two Sisters with a Hawk Watching," in *The Closed Eye Open*

"Toccata and Fugue," in *The Plentitudes*

"Parallel Octaves," in *Digging Through the Fat*

"Echo of Exploding Bombs," in *Digging through the Fat*

"Interrupted Play" was first published as "Change of Life Baby," in *Inkwell Journal*

"Calming Properties of Ice Cream" was first published as "Love in the Time of COVID," in *Birdland Journal*

"Surprising Effects of a Dewy Grass Bath," in *The Potato Soup Journal*

"Ghosts in the Grand Wardrobe," in *Smoky Blue Literary and Arts Magazine*

"Fallen Star," in *Birdland Journal*

"Birds on the Water" was first published as "Goran Holds His Breath," in *Shenandoah*

"Miles to Go," in *The Plentitudes*

"Ultimate Mystery" was first published as "Change in Breathing," by *The Examined Life Journal*

About the Author

Jeanne Althouse has been writing stories about secrets since her mother gave her a journal when she was eight. In search of mysteries, she has traveled to Narnia, flown through a Wrinkle in Time, and shared hot chocolate with Atticus and Scout. Her therapist has probed the question of why she is driven to write these tales of hidden sins and desires, but after years of expensive sessions, the reason remains a secret.

Her stories have been published in numerous literary journals, two chapbooks, and twice nominated for a Pushcart. She lives in Palo Alto, California with her favorite husband, and snow tigers Sacha and Zara.

Made in the USA
Middletown, DE
25 September 2023

39293063R00066